Montrose scowled dark enough to crack the earth. "What makes you think I want to go through that hell again?"

Ophelia wasn't the least bit afraid of his scowls by now. "You have a duty to marry, and you know it. I am sure, given time and the right circumstances, you will easily find the perfect bride. Your duchess is just waiting to be swept off her feet somewhere. Besides, you'd never let your cousin inherit Sherringford for the lack of a son."

His face darkened even more.

She charged on. "So, you will need a new bride…and perhaps a little practice with the ladies."

He frowned. "Practice at what? I'm hardly an innocent."

Ophelia blushed. "And I'm a married woman with a broad mind. You should seduce me."

His face slowly turned an alarming shade of purple.

Heather Boyd

USA TODAY BESTSELLING AUTHOR

His Perfect Bride

Distinguished Rogues

Chapter One

August, 1815

Ophelia Shaw set her hand upon Mr. Drayton's sleeve, grateful for his support as she hobbled along on her wooden foot and bamboo cane, but aware her stomach was bound in knots. Ophelia's anxiety had a lot to do with the man at her side…but also with another, currently absent gentleman's likely reaction to a question she'd been recently asked.

"I very much enjoyed your sermon today," she assured the vicar.

Stephen Drayton was not much taller than herself, gray-haired and pleasant to look upon but not handsome. He was at least fifteen years older, though she had never dared ask his exact age. Stephen Drayton had sad brown eyes that perfectly matched the equally somber attire required for his profession as a country vicar.

He had asked her to marry him last week after a subtle inquiry about her place in the duke's household. Honestly, she couldn't have been more surprised.

Drayton was a good man, and yet Ophelia harbored doubts about accepting his offer of marriage before the Duke of Montrose returned. Her late husband's cousin might not like the connection. And Ophelia couldn't picture herself as a proper and prim country vicar's wife, even if such a marriage might be her only choice for a secure future.

Ophelia could never imagine sharing the marriage bed with Stephen Drayton, either. He didn't excite her passions in the least.

Drayton chuckled. "Are you sure? I could have sworn I heard snoring from your side of the church," he teased.

He was amusing at times. Mr. Drayton liked to tease her, but only when no one could hear him do it. She laughed softly. "Snoring?"

"Delicate snoring. Tiny sounds. Though perhaps, now I think about it, Mrs. Mason was sitting a distance behind you. I always manage to put her to sleep with my sermons."

Ophelia liked that Drayton's offer of marriage and her failure to answer in the affirmative immediately had not affected their interactions thus far. Marriage was a big decision to make a second time round. The first time, Ophelia had jumped in without any real consideration for the consequences or knowing the full character of the man she would wed. She'd told Mr. Drayton she'd give him an answer soon. But as the days passed, she was no closer to knowing what to do.

Drayton was too polite to complain that a woman her age ought to know her own mind by now.

"Your sermon has given me much to think about."

Mr. Drayton's eyes lit up. "I had hoped so."

She shivered. "Montrose will not be home with his bride for some weeks yet."

Mr. Drayton nodded slowly. "His bringing Sherringford a new mistress has everyone excited. More than a few widows and unwed ladies are put out that Montrose had not considered them for the role. He's taken us all by surprise. Speaking of marriage, have you given any more thought to *my* proposal?"

So much for giving her time.

Drayton's proposal had been contingent on the duke not needing her anymore to run his household, a responsibility she enjoyed and that gave her purpose. She had become quite fond of her new home, and the duke too. Not that Montrose could have any clue he was so often thoughts or like that she foolishly imagined him in her bed some nights.

That was one of the reasons she hadn't dismissed Mr. Drayton's proposal out of hand. She was also aware that the expense of a wife, one with her physical limitations, would put a strain on Drayton's pocketbook, more so than if he married someone more able-bodied who didn't need a maid's help for almost everything.

Stephen Drayton had thought they would be good company for each other. He'd spoken of a quiet life of prayer and doing good for others.

To be completely honest, Ophelia worried that she'd grow bored with such a life. She may not be the devil-may-care debutant of her youth, but that didn't mean she didn't want to still be in the thick of things and live a passionate life.

Stephen was well informed but not brilliant. He didn't fascinate her like other men could when he spoke, but he did not put her to sleep during his sermons, either.

Yet if not a marriage to this man, and if Montrose had no more use for her, what would she do with her life? Ophelia had done nothing but wonder about that since the moment she'd first arrived at Sherringford—newly widowed and unable to move about easily.

It had been a relief that Montrose had charged in and made decisions, as her husband had complained he was wont to do. Montrose had come as soon as he'd learned of her husband's passing and her injuries, though Paul and Montrose had not been close cousins.

Upon waking after the accident, Ophelia had become aware of a male presence beside her sickbed, though his head was bowed. At first, she'd mistaken the man for her husband and had threaded her fingers into his soft dark hair.

When Montrose had lifted his face instead, blinking his sleepy green eyes, her heart had started to pound in shock and panic.

Her husband had been dead a week by then, Montrose had told her brusquely, and was already buried, his life stolen by the same carriage accident that had crushed her foot beyond repair and required an amputation.

It was very likely only because of Montrose that she was alive to this day. He'd browbeaten the surgeon and maids into doing their best work and stayed to oversee her recovery.

He'd refused to allow her to give up, too. She remembered his insistence and the words he'd uttered over and over each night, when she couldn't sleep for the pain.

Stay with me.

She had. Her recovery had taken months. While she recovered, Montrose settled her husband's debts and packed up their modest belongings, sending them on to Sherringford, his ducal estate. Ophelia had been relieved to have him take charge because, aside from her husband's family, she had no one else to turn to.

But seeing Montrose's severe expression at her bedside each morning had been a somewhat unnerving experience for those first few weeks.

Ophelia had only met Montrose once before the accident, a month after she'd married his cousin. She remembered how awkward she'd felt, and self-conscious around the austere and clearly disapproving duke. He hadn't helped to make her feel at ease around him, either, being curt and seemingly impossible to please. He also never smiled.

But from the day she'd woken after the accident, he'd become her lifeline.

When she announced her belief that she was fit to travel, the duke had insisted on a delay of another week and then borne her home to Sherringford in grand style—traveling in easy stages that had still left her exhausted each night when they'd taken shelter at a succession of inns. She had slept most of the trip, reclining in Montrose's well-padded carriage during the day. He'd sat across from her the whole way to Sherringford, hardly taking his eyes from her, it had seemed.

And then, once at Sherringford, he'd abandoned her to the care of an army of servants, and she'd hardly seen him but once a day as he enquired how she fared.

She owed him so much, and had no means to ever repay him. She also had no explanation for why he'd taken such a personal interest in her recovery at the beginning, when she'd suspected early on in her marriage that he hadn't even liked her. But when she'd become restless with her confinement and able to move around his vast home on crutches or in a wheeled chair, he'd suddenly offered her the challenge of running his household, with a battalion of servants to do her bidding.

Her new role had helped Ophelia set aside her grief, and also gave her an excuse to get out of bed each morning.

She'd assumed, though it was never spelled out, that it was only ever to be a short-term arrangement. He'd said nothing about making the position permanent. But weeks had dragged into months with no discussion of the future until one day, out of the blue, he'd confided that he would make a change in his life, and thus hers as well.

His announcement that he would be going to London to

marry had come as a complete shock. She recalled standing frozen in his presence, not knowing what to say, and feeling like her world was about to end all over again.

The day of his departure she recalled with perfect clarity. She'd stood with the servants on the drive early one morning as his carriage rolled away and had started to weep because he was leaving her behind. Ophelia had quickly brushed away her tears before anyone saw of course, and had turned for the manor, determined to make the house perfect for his return, and for the future Duchess of Montrose.

But during the long nights and endless days of his absence she had worried about him. Worried more than she felt she should.

"I have been thinking of the future, of course," she told Mr. Drayton with a sincere smile. "Until I am certain of the duke's wishes for the future, I cannot yet answer. Leaving could inconvenience him and his new wife. I owe him so much after all the kindness he's shown me."

Marriage was a big step for a woman—especially for one with only one foot.

Drayton was not the sort of man Ophelia would once have paid any attention to. However, she was not a respectably dowered young lady anymore with the world at her feet. Especially not now; she did not even possess two feet to stand upon. She did not hope to make a better marriage...but wondered if she had to make any at all.

Drayton picked up her free hand and clasped it firmly in his. She noted his hands were dry and rather soft. "Well, no matter what happens, always remember you were a welcome addition to our society when you came. Your kindness to us all has impressed us. Especially me. You have done a lot of good here in Montrose's name. That means a lot to our little community."

She blushed at his praise. She did have a tiny bit of influence over the Duke of Montrose, but that would likely end when he married. She hoped the future duchess could persuade him the way she had, and do better, too.

Montrose had confessed he'd chosen a lady of great fortune but had never been persuaded to describe the woman in any detail. Ophelia assumed her young, fashionable, and very beautiful. Like all the wives of great men should be.

The toe of her false foot caught on the edge of a flagstone, and she would have fallen flat on her face if not for Drayton catching her and pulling her close.

"I have you," he promised. "Hold tight to my arm and I'll help you to the carriage."

"I'm fine," she promised, pushing aside his assistance quickly, flustered as much by her tripping as by Drayton's nearness.

"You're doing very well. So much improved since the day we first met, my dear."

Ophelia almost winced at the endearment that rolled off his tongue. She really should have given Drayton an answer, but she had the added excuse of Montrose's extended absence to delay giving it. Living upon Montrose's generosity and charity meant she'd been able to forget certain hard truths about her situation. She would need to learn the state of her financial affairs before she committed herself to any match.

Ophelia's knowledge of finance was very limited, a fault of no one's but her own and her rash impulse to elope with her late husband, allowing him to keep her in the dark.

"You are very kind. I am sure Montrose will discuss how things will change when his bride arrives."

Mr. Drayton nodded, his fingers returning to claim hers. "If you need someone to confide in after, I'm available to you at any time," he promised. "I know how distressing talking to him can be."

Ophelia pulled her hand back. Too much familiarity could have tongues wagging. "The Duke of Montrose has been nothing but kind to me."

"Of course," Drayton said soothingly. "You are kind to overlook his bad manners to others. I'm glad to hear, at least to you, he can remember to be gallant."

Ophelia wouldn't stand about to hear anyone disparage Montrose. "Yes, he can be cutting to those who displease him. That is the way of duke's. Good day to you, Mr. Drayton."

"Mrs. Shaw," Drayton murmured with an apologetic smile, as if realizing he'd gone too far in his critique of her cousin by marriage. "Might I have the honor of assisting you into your carriage."

"I am capable of the feat alone now, thank you," she assured him.

Most of the time.

She hobbled away from Drayton before he could detain her with further conversation.

Montrose's grooms loitered by the second-best carriage not far away, partaking of the sunshine instead of the sermons inside the stuffy church house. She did not blame them. She had avoided church most of her life once, too.

But soon after her arrival, Ophelia became aware that people of the district viewed her with a certain degree of hostility and suspicion, and gossiped about the arrangement she had managing the Sherringford great house. She had come to church as soon as she was fit enough, though Montrose disagreed that she ever needed to bother. He didn't seem to realize or care that her presence in a bachelor's household might be considered scandalous. Ophelia had done all she could to project an image of dignity and decorum while in society.

At the door to the open carriage, she faced the interior with weary resignation. This was the tricky part. Climbing up two steps into a carriage was not always simple, but she refused to be lifted in anymore. No matter how well-intentioned that help might seem, Ophelia was tired of always feeling embarrassed afterward.

A pair of grooms rushed to stand at each side of her, ready to catch her should she become unbalanced and start to topple.

She handed one her cane and took hold of the newly added rails at each side of the carriage doorway and hopped up. On the first step, she wobbled. On the second, she grinned, but the harder step was still to come. She had to stretch farther forward without anything substantial to hold onto and hop inside to finally reach the carriage seat.

As she made an attempt, she wobbled—and then someone grasped her firmly around the waist from behind and steadied her.

"I have you."

Ophelia fairly flew across the carriage then and landed horribly awry across one seat. Her skirts became wrapped around her legs, making it hard to straighten up with any sort of ladylike precision. She was embarrassed, her cheeks flaming.

The hands around her waist, the voice, had belonged to the Duke of Montrose.

The duke was back.

The carriage shook, and then gentle hands lifted her up and deposited her on the seat properly. She looked up at the Duke of Montrose's stern face in utter surprise as he settled into the opposite seat.

"You are home," she noted, then blushed even more. She

had thought of him every day since he'd left her behind. It was such a relief to see him again that she fought to contain her overwhelming happiness. But contain it she must because the duke would likely not appreciate her making a fuss over him.

"Indeed. I should have known I would find you here again amongst the grasping rabble," Montrose grumbled.

Montrose was not religious, they had that in common, and he had little time for the vicar, too. He'd never forbidden her from attending services on Sundays, but he never looked happy when she was on her way out the door.

He threw a thunderous scowl at the lingering grooms, who scrambled to return to their positions posthaste. Only with his nod of approval did the carriage begin to roll forward, driving them back toward the Sherringford Estate.

Ophelia wet her lips, suddenly nervous of him. "I wasn't expecting you for some weeks yet."

He grunted, scowled darkly, and Ophelia knew better than to ask another question straight away. The duke was a moody man. He could terrify his servants just by dropping a book too loudly.

She glanced out the window and spotted his larger closed traveling carriage following them home. So, he was only just back. Had he brought his bride with him already?

She lifted her hand, prepared to wave to the new duchess, until Montrose spoke.

"Don't bother. There's no one in the carriage," he told her.

Ophelia met his gaze slowly, astonished by the news. Montrose had promised to return with his bride. He had sounded so sure that he would be a married man the next time they saw each other. "What do you mean?"

He scowled again. "She changed her mind."

"Oh," Ophelia said slowly—and was ashamed to realize

she felt immense relief at the news Montrose was not married, or about to be. And then anger on his behalf. "But why?"

"Isn't it explanation enough that she released me from the engagement?" he snapped, and then his jaw clenched. "I don't want to talk about it."

Ophelia bit her tongue. She wouldn't be getting any more conversation out of Montrose until he was calmer. She'd made a study of his moods and behaviors over the past months. If she pried, he'd throw up his defenses, and he'd tell her nothing at all.

Chapter Two

Harry saw Ophelia's disappointment, but wouldn't change his mind and reveal the whole story of his time away. Some humiliations could not be shared…especially not with someone like *her*. And it would do no good to dwell on his mistake. He'd left a bachelor and returned the same.

Nothing had changed.

The journey home from the village gave him ample opportunity to observe Ophelia Shaw's ever-changing expressions. She was worried. Though about what, he couldn't tell. Was it that he'd returned without a bride, or that he'd returned to the estate at all?

Her lips pressed together in a tight line, and that signified to him that she had something grim on her mind. During the whole of her time confined to her sickbed, she'd worn that exact expression many times. She never would tell him what she worried about then, and he'd learned not to pester her for explanations now. There was a distance between them—a vast chasm that might never be spanned. There had to be, too, though he regretted that he'd just snapped at her.

However, he would not tell her how badly his time in London had really gone.

He should never have bothered trying to find a bride when the sweet and gentle woman before him was everything he'd ever wanted…but couldn't admit to.

She was his cousin's widowed bride. Grieving for the love

of her life still. A man who had been Harry's exact opposite in every way.

Ophelia was perfect—elegant and serene, vastly intelligent, though she downplayed that before him still.

She was much too good for an ogre, so he kept his admiration well-hidden and maintained a respectable distance at all times. She'd been hurt enough by the accident, by her late husband's careless disregard for her safety, and Harry wanted to have the privilege of looking after her for the rest of his days. He'd even concocted a scheme to occupy *her* days, claiming that he needed her assistance to run Sherringford.

To his surprise, she'd thrived on the challenge of running his household, even going so far as to involve herself with the wider world around the estate. She was admired and respected. Harry was in awe of her.

Just then, a change in the scenery caught his eye as they passed into open farmland. One of the smaller tenant cottages seemed to be swarming with men. "What's going on there?"

She shrugged. "I'm told there was a great cracking heard one evening a few nights ago, and when morning came, the wall had fallen outward."

Harry peered at the scene again. Of sound timber construction, the cottage had no right to simply fall apart on a whim. "I can't believe that."

"Neither can anyone else," Ophelia muttered. "What matters is that the house is under repair, and all is well again."

He sat back, peering at her. "What are you not telling me?"

A stain of color began to climb her cheeks, and she looked down at her hands. "It was too much to hope the matter could be resolved without your involvement. I fear you will be made unhappy by the news."

"But not with the teller of the tale," he promised. "Now, what really happened?"

She sighed heavily. "You are right. The cottage did not simply start falling apart. It had help. The Johnson brothers got into a bit of a row a few nights ago."

He leaned forward. "How much of a row?"

"No one died," she promised with a wince. "But Mrs. Nash has a broken arm."

Harry ground his teeth. Maggie Nash was an older woman, and slow-moving. She also tended to involve herself in other people's affairs. He wouldn't be surprised to learn she had been in the thick of the row, hoping her presence would cool the hot tempers. Usually, her meddling turned out well. She'd never been harmed before that he knew of.

He turned to the driver. "The Nash farm. Now."

When he turned back to Ophelia, she was biting her lip again.

He stretched out a hand, palm facing her, hoping the gesture would reassure her. "I'll speak with Mrs. Nash and then deal with that rabble once and for all."

She winced again. "I have something to confess, and you might not like it. I didn't want the matter to spoil your home-coming with your bride, so something had to be done to stop the quarreling pair starting up again. I have overstepped my duties, but I came up with a punishment for them in your absence."

He looked at her in surprise. "What did you do?"

She pointed out the carriage. "You'll see in a moment."

They turned into the Nash drive and headed for the cottage that was set in the midst of open fields. Maggie Nash was a sweet lady. She'd once been a maid at Sherringford but had been unfairly dismissed by Harry's late father. Harry wouldn't ever admit it to anyone, but he had a soft spot for the woman. She had been kind to him as a boy. She'd married a local, and her husband was a decent sort. Quiet, just the way Harry liked his neighbors.

He easily saw the pair since they were sitting out in the sun together, studying their land as they often did on warm summer days. Everything seemed as he'd left it. "What am I not seeing?"

"Look there," Ophelia murmured, pointing away from the Nashes. "Out in the field."

Harry squinted. "The field is being plowed."

"And the Johnson brothers are taking turns at being the horse. They have that whole field to do, and then the next one, too. After that, they're promised to labor at the mill, sawing lumber that will one day become the furniture they destroyed in their own cottage."

Harry considered what he knew of their situation. The Johnson brothers had recently come into some money and suddenly thought themselves above their neighbors. New coats, extra servants. Strutting about the village as if they owned the place. "That's hot and dirty work for a pair of would-be toffs."

"Exactly." Ophelia smiled serenely. "If they behave like animals, I say we treat them as such. They offered to pay compensation, but I knew Mr. Nash would never have taken a penny of it. So, I made another suggestion, and everyone agreed. The pair have buckled down to their punishment with only a bit of grumbling about it now and then. I hope the hard work will remind them to respect what they have and to take more care around their elders."

Harry rubbed his hand over his jaw. It wasn't exactly how he would have punished the pair, but he couldn't think of a single objection to her plan to knock them down a peg or two on the local social ladder. It might just improve their manners faster than tossing them out on their rears—which is what he would have done that very day most likely.

The carriage stopped near the Nashes, and he stepped out. Ophelia remained seated, as he expected her to do.

The pair bounced up, though he noted Mrs. Nash clutched her arm to prevent any jostling. She curtsied to him while her husband touched his cap. "Your grace, what an honor."

"Mr. Nash. I've just heard what transpired." He looked down on Maggie Nash, concerned about her in a way he was for very few people. "Are you all right, Maggie?"

"I'm fine," she promised with a smile, then drew closer. She set her hand lightly on his sleeve. "Just a little bump. Don't worry about me now."

He shook his head. He worried, but he rarely showed it. People claimed him cold, unlovable, but Maggie knew better. And she had always shown him affection. That was the reason his father had actually dismissed her from Sherringford. Harry had not been allowed to care about anyone as a boy, and when he'd been seen laughing with Maggie, a maid, over some trifling matter, she'd been dismissed that very night.

He'd learned not to laugh with the servants after that.

He covered her hand briefly with his. "A broken arm is no trifling matter."

"I'll heal soon enough." She pulled away. "Don't let this spoil your homecoming, your grace. It's good to have you back where you belong."

"Thank you."

She curtsied, and then backed away.

Her husband gestured Harry to join him in a stroll toward the pair plowing the field.

"Is the punishment to your taste, Nash?"

"Vastly, your grace," he promised. "After all the help my

Maggie has given to the raising of their younger sister, they deserve worse."

Harry offered a rumbling sound of assent, but he did not offer an alternative.

Nash was much older than Harry, twenty years Maggie's senior, too. Over the years, Harry had learned to trust his opinions, and even sought them out occasionally.

Nash smiled. "My Maggie is all right. Just a bit of pain now and again. Mrs. Shaw saw to the bone being set herself and sent a maid from the estate to help with any chores. I appreciate her insistence the Johnsons not get off so lightly as being rendered homeless for what they did."

In the field, the Johnsons had stopped to yell at each other. Harry frowned. "It seems they have not yet seen the error of their ways."

"A prolonged punishment is just the thing then," Nash decided. "It's been a vastly entertaining few days watching them trying to work together. Get back to it, you drunken sots," Nash suddenly shouted.

Harry folded his arms across his chest, glowering at the distant pair in distaste. "So, they were cup-shot?"

"Nasty night all round. Their sister came to us in a right state. That's how we knew something was amiss. I swear if Mrs. Shaw hadn't suddenly appeared, too, there would have been bloodshed. Nothing quiets an argument faster than Mrs. Shaw shuffling into a room."

Harry grunted. Her presence soothed *him*, too. Ophelia had a knack for getting people to do what she wanted without even saying a word. He probably did owe her some sort of explanation for his bad mood, but he'd pick his time well to tell her. He'd wait till he wasn't as angry about it anymore. "Well, as long as you're satisfied."

"Indeed, I am." Nash turned to look behind them and grinned. "Thick as thieves again, that pair."

Harry looked behind him, too. Maggie Nash and Ophelia appeared deep in conversation, though Ophelia remained in the carriage for the conversation. They had taken to each other almost from their first meeting, and Harry approved their friendship since Maggie was a woman of sense. "Yes."

"She'll perk up, now you're back."

Harry sighed. "Maggie has no reason to worry about me. I'm not a little boy anymore."

"I was speaking of Mrs. Shaw. If you ask me, she's been a bit low these past weeks. Now you're back, I expect she'll be her happy self again."

He saw nothing different in Ophelia's manner. "What reason could she have to be unhappy?"

"Alone in that big house without you."

Harry tried not to roll his eyes. "There are at least forty staff at Sherringford ready to wait on her, and no doubt Maggie has visited."

"It's not the same as having you around, and you know it."

Harry frowned. He'd wondered if the quiet of Sherringford would dissatisfy Ophelia in the end. She'd had a more exciting life, married to his cousin Paul. She'd traveled extensively throughout England with him and had enjoyed visits from friends whenever they'd taken on a lease of a house. Since coming to Sherringford, Ophelia had been nearly closeted, with only the local families for amusement. "Do you think I should hire a woman for her?"

Nash chuckled. "A companion would only get in your way. But I do think you should do something about that torch you're carrying for her one of these days."

Harry stilled—and then pretended he hadn't heard Nash.

"Come now, lad. It's been plain as day to anyone who

knows you well that you care about her." Nash smiled know-ingly. "And where is that bride you promised to bring home with you, eh?"

Harry licked his lips. Nervous that a neighbor had noticed his interest in Ophelia. He'd thought he'd hid his feeling better. "Of course I have an interest in her. She's my cousin's widow."

"That's not the reason you're interested. She's a fine woman." Nash glanced at his workers in the field, put his hands up to cup his mouth, and shouted out again, "Well, don't just stand there, Johnsons. Field's not going to plow itself, and you've another to do yet." Nash faced Harry and grinned. "If you don't speak up, someone will try to take her off your hands."

Harry knew that, but he doubted any would be successful. Not unless they were like Paul—outgoing, funny, adventurous.

Harry scowled at Nash, but his neighbor merely chuckled. "Now, don't take a set against me for speaking out of turn. You need the nudge. You've been happier since she came to stay. Now, it's time I convinced Maggie to rest her arm, and you'd best get Mrs. Shaw home before she takes a chill."

Harry glanced up at the sky. The day was perfect in every respect. Not a cloud in the heavens and warm.

When he glanced at Nash, the man was struggling not to grin. "It could rain."

"Nash, you are tilting at windmills."

"You don't say."

Despite the perfect weather that had no chance of turning bad, Harry hurried to the carriage and the lovely woman waiting for him.

Mrs. Nash was still whispering to her through the open carriage door, but she stopped when they saw him returning.

Harry expected the whispers and the pitying looks to continue in the coming weeks. At least they would not talk about him dangling after his cousin's widow, as Nash had just done.

Ophelia had most likely told Maggie he'd returned unmarried. Hell, Mr. Nash had guessed, and Harry hadn't even said a word. Harry would prefer the version *he* wanted known about his failure to marry, rather than a wild embellishment the gossips might concoct. Tomorrow, he'd tell Ophelia what she needed to know, and that would truly be the end of the matter, he hoped. He'd settle back into his usual routine and spend his spare moments keeping an eye on Ophelia from a distance—or reminding the servants to do so.

Harry climbed in opposite Ophelia and waved the Nashes goodbye.

When the Nash farm had fallen well behind, he turned to her. Ophelia fascinated him, though he'd always tried to hide it well. If Nash had figured it out, no doubt others might have, too. He would have to be more careful to hide his partiality in the future.

He frowned. He might have to avoid her again. Something he found difficult to do. But from tomorrow onward, not today. "You did the right thing about the Johnsons, though it remains to be seen if it's a cure for their quarreling."

"Thank you for saying so, your grace. One can only hope they can be civilized."

They were silent for the remainder of the journey. Harry ran the events of the past weeks over in his mind, deciding what to leave out of the telling. In retrospect, he'd rushed the proposal. He'd just wanted it over and done with so he could come home again.

At the front steps of the manor, he found the odious vicar

waiting to greet him. The damn man rushed right up to his carriage door, too.

"Your grace," Mr. Stephen Drayton exclaimed with a condescending smile that never failed to irritate Harry. "I'm sorry to have missed you in the village. Welcome home and may I be the first to offer my congratulations."

"Drayton," he said shortly. The last thing he needed today was a pompous windbag darkening his doorstep. "Make an appointment with my secretary for later in the week."

"Actually, it was Mrs. Shaw I came to see."

Harry frowned severely. Drayton had just assaulted Ophelia with a Sunday sermon and should have no further business monopolizing her attention today. He held out his arm to her, to prevent her from having to agree to stay. "Mrs. Shaw has duties to attend to. You'll have to come back another time."

Next decade would suite Harry perfectly well. Ophelia could never say no to anyone. Drayton was always wailing about his orphans or some other lost cause. And then Ophelia would tell him about it, and by the end of the discussion, Harry's purse would be lighter.

Harry was relieved when Ophelia apologized to the vicar, and he subtly urged her toward the door to Sherringford with as much haste as possible for her. She did have business inside, but it had nothing to do with the management of the house. Harry dismissed Drayton from his mind, as well as with a wave of his hand, and drew her inside.

Harry's time in London hadn't been an entire waste. He'd made a few purchases—all of them for Ophelia.

When she saw the crates and boxes piled up on the floor in the great hall, she gasped in distress. "Oh, no. You made purchases for her?"

"Good God, no. These are for you," he promised, pacing

around the pile. Seeing his purchases all stacked in one place made him realize he might have gone a too far with his spending on Ophelia though he regretted nothing. He hoped she would not attempt to refuse his gifts too strenuously.

"Mine? But it's not my birthday for another month."

He dismissed her words with a flick of his hand. "I've not the desire to return to Town again for some time, so this will have to do you for the birthday and Christmas gifts as well."

Harry had had ample time to become acquainted with the limited scope of Ophelia's possessions during her long confinement and her subsequent move to Sherringford. There were a great many things a lady needed, though Ophelia had never asked for any of them in all the time she'd been under his roof. He was tired of seeing her in the same plain gowns she'd worn since her accident. The severe black of mourning had been recently replaced with decidedly unpretty gowns she'd already owned. The gowns his cousin had provided had clearly cost but a few shillings, when it should have been pounds spent instead.

So, Harry had taken it upon himself to compile a long list and send his London housekeeper—who seemed to his eye to be of similar proportions and height—out on a spending spree on Ophelia's behalf. He was well pleased with the results.

Modest jewels as well as undergarments had been discreetly purchased by him. It was a bit torturous to imagine Ophelia wearing his silk chemise about Stapleton, under his very nose, but if he couldn't have her, he would still treat her to the very best his money could buy. There were also bolts of fabrics and laces, gloves and hats for her to choose from. Ready-made gowns for both daywear and evening enter-tainments.

She'd started going out a bit before he'd gone to London, and it seemed to him then that other people were good for keeping her spirits up…except for the vicar, of course. Harry would never approve of him, though Ophelia was more tolerant.

There were enough bits and bobs from several haberdashery shops to keep her well amused at her sewing when the colder months descended upon them and she couldn't venture out.

He edged away. "Give away what you don't want."

"I couldn't do that." She sighed heavily. "Oh, my dear duke, what a fool she was to refuse you. You've been too generous."

Ophelia moved toward him suddenly, and stopped very close. She stretched up toward his face with her lips puckered. Harry was a fair bit taller than her and, despite the awkwardness, leaned his cheek down to her. "It was nothing."

Her lips were soft on his skin, and they lingered while the scent of her perfume assaulted his starved senses.

He loved her so very much, and he was grateful for any excuse to spoil her.

"You shouldn't have gone to so much trouble, but thank you for thinking of me when you must have had so much else on your mind."

Yes. He'd been lavishing attention on the wrong woman, when the one he wanted he'd left behind. Had Ophelia really been lonely without him? Looking at her now, he couldn't quite believe Nashes claim. "We'll talk again tomorrow," he promised as he edged toward the door again.

Her soft smile nearly undid him. "I'll look forward to it."

Chapter Three

"My goodness, his grace must have opened his pocketbook wide to pay for all this," the senior downstairs maid, Gertie Fritz, exclaimed loudly.

Ophelia agreed, and was a little embarrassed by all the riches that had been carelessly heaped upon her. They were in her sitting room the next morning, the only space large enough to contain all of the duke's gifts, while the maids were helping her find places to fit the duke's unexpected largess. She was even more stunned by the many and varied items than when she'd first seen it all lumped together in crates in the front hall yesterday. He must have spent a fortune on her, and she'd certainly never expected him to. "I don't think I'll need anything else new for the next ten years," she murmured.

"Maybe only seven." Lilly Watson, another maid, grinned. "Even with only one foot, shoes will wear out the way you try to run around the grounds."

Ophelia chuckled. She wanted to be the way she'd once been—agile and graceful. Full of energy and life. That was harder now with a wooden foot, but not impossible.

Gertie held up one of the bolts of fine silk cloth against her body and turned to show Ophelia. The color was glorious. Dark pink shot through with black. "Now that's a truly remarkable color," she noted.

"It'll make a lovely evening gown," Gertie assured her. "If only we had a London seamstress to do it justice."

Ophelia would have to employ the local seamstress and

hope for the best. She was rubbish at making any clothes that fit well for herself. "Well, there'll be no balls at Sherringford for perhaps another year now, I expect."

"Not unless his grace finds another bride from among the local nobility. If he does marry one of them, and the nuptials are held here, you could wear this for the wedding party."

Montrose had to marry. There was no way he could avoid it. He needed an heir of his own and a wife in his bed to get one. She tried not to think of that aspect of him being married too often. "You assume I'd be invited to any wedding," she said as she admired a new shawl.

"Of course, you will attend," Gertie chided. "How could you not? His grace depends upon you. Do you really think he would have bought you all these luxurious fabrics if he hadn't wanted to see you finely dressed in them?"

She hadn't been wanted in London this season to meet Montrose's intended bride. Maybe if she'd been there in London, things would have turned out differently for him. She might have helped smooth his way.

Or would the lady have run screaming from her disability?

That was Ophelia's greatest fear—that her amputated limb would horrify his new wife and set her apart. People who looked different were shunned by the healthy. She'd known that even before her carriage accident.

Maybe that was why Montrose hadn't taken her to London with him. He'd not want people staring or talking about her injury when the spotlight should, of course, be firmly placed on the new Duchess of Montrose.

Ophelia sighed. "At first, I wondered if all of this was meant for his bride. The one who cried off."

"Well, *this* certainly could not be," Gertie exclaimed, holding up a new boot, made of tan leather and stitched with gold thread. She already had several that strapped around her upper calf to hold them in place. The duke seemed committed to finding just the right one for her.

Ophelia rushed to see the new boot. She hefted it in her hand and turned it over. "Similar but very much lighter, I think."

"Perhaps you won't tire so quickly."

"That would be nice," Ophelia murmured and set it aside. She'd try it out later and see what adjustments must be made for a comfortable fit.

"If he said all this were for you, then I'd believe him. Our duke does not mince words or spend his coin unwisely."

"I know that is true." She smiled quickly. For some things, Montrose's wallet was clenched tighter than a drum. Yet, for other causes, Ophelia could appeal to his generosity if she phrased her requests a certain way. He was, at least, always willing to listen to her opinion even if he did not always agree with it.

"Look at this. Silk!" Gertie exclaimed as she held up a delicate white chemise and wiggled it in the air at Ophelia. "The duke has exceptionally good taste in undergarments."

Blushing now, Ophelia quickly snatched the chemise away from Gertie. She neatly folded the item to place with a number of other undergarments he'd given her. "I'm sure he had a servant make those purchases."

Her late husband's cousin was a confusing man to Ophelia. Experience had proved that Montrose did nothing as expected. He was frequently moody, irritable with the staff, and he never explained himself to anyone, least of all her. She'd tried to become his confidant, to make herself useful instead of the burden she was, and had been rebuffed many times. Now, he'd done all this. How could he be so kind and generous but always seem uncomfortable when she tried to thank him?

The woman who'd cried off from marrying him was undoubtedly a fool. She had missed her chance to live a comfortable life with the Duke of Montrose.

"Ooh, there he is, back from his morning ride," Lilly exclaimed, staring out the window.

Gertie rushed to join her.

The maids sighed in such a way that made their admiration plain. Montrose might have a temper, but the sight of him striding about the estate, all brooding good looks and windswept from a ride, tended to send the female servants into a bit of a swoon. Ophelia understood his appeal, even as she tried to discourage the others from talking about him that way around her.

Secretly, she enjoyed the view, too. Montrose cut quite a handsome figure. His deep gruff voice put wicked thoughts in her head that she could only relieve at night alone in the bed he'd given her.

Ophelia joined them at the window in time to watch the duke dismount some distance away. Yes, he had a truly remarkable presence. He was a hard man to ignore. His movements were smooth and capable, his stride unhurried as he led his horse toward the stable and when he disappeared, she sighed too. "He's in a good mood," she observed.

The maids turned from the window as well with another round of heavy sighs. "Thank heavens for that. When we learned he'd returned from London empty-handed, we feared we'd have to tiptoe around him for weeks."

"He's every right to be angry," Ophelia chided.

"Oh, we agree, but it's always awkward when he storms about the place. Nothing pleases him."

Every servant at Sherringford knew to scatter when Montrose was in a bad mood. Even Ophelia had considered it once or twice. But since her husband's death, Montrose was the only close family she really had. There were other cousins, but they lived far away and were also dependent on Montrose's generosity.

Montrose made her life easier to bear in so many ways, and the least she could do was make an attempt to soothe his temper if she could.

He'd taken her in, made sure she had the necessities of life, and more now, but never shown any sign of wanting to confide in her about his concerns. She lived on pins and needles that he'd grow tired of offering his charity to a nearly useless woman, and send her away from the home she'd grown to love.

Her only choice for a settled life might be to accept Mr. Drayton's offer of marriage, even if she already knew she could never love the man.

Ophelia picked up a hat, one with a wide brim. It was too big for her head but charming. Although she hated to do it, she set it aside with the other things that didn't fit her.

Gertie snatched up the hat immediately and tried it on. "It doesn't fit me, either."

It fit Lilly to perfection, though.

"You may have that," Ophelia murmured, hoping Montrose really wouldn't mind seeing it on another woman's head in the future.

She dug a little more into the pile and pulled out a small square box. Inside was a delicate gold timepiece attached to a pin and chain. It was exquisite and costly, and she loved it on sight.

She set down the new timepiece and fumbled for her husband's old timepiece that she carried concealed in her pocket. She'd bought it for her husband for their first anniversary. She had scrimped and saved enough to buy the very best she could afford.

At the time of their accident, Paul Shaw had been consulting this pocket watch. He had been in a hurry to get to where they were going by a certain time.

When she put Paul's watch beside Montrose's, it looked decidedly shabby, but it held so many memories Most happy but some bittersweet. She hesitated for a moment…and then affixed the new watch to her gown with its shiny pin and chain.

Paul was gone.

She packed Paul's timepiece away in a drawer, where the past ought to remain. She had to think of the future now.

"That's lovely," Gertie murmured, coming up to stand beside her and admire her gift.

"It is." Ophelia checked the time. "Practical, too. You two can return to your usual duties now."

"Very good, Mrs. Shaw." The pair curtsied and hurried away.

Ophelia lingered beside the fabrics. In truth, they were much too elegant for the country, unless the duke entertained more often. She ran her fingers over the silks, enjoying the rare luxury. She'd never had a silk gown made for her before. Her husband's pocketbook hadn't allowed for too many frivolous indulgences.

She held a length of fabric up to her body and limped to the mirror.

She arranged the folds into a pleasing shape but wished she could have a more experienced modiste to advise her how it might be made into a gown suitable for the evening. Something that would please Montrose to see her in, too.

She ran her hand down her body again, imagining him touching her body while she wore a beautiful gown made from silk. A blush warmed her cheeks as her fingers brushed perilously close to her mons. She jerked her fingers away and started folding the fabric into a neat bundle. Too many times her mind wandered to the intimacies best satisfied in the bedchamber and lately included Montrose lavishing her with affection.

It was torture thinking of him that way yet she could not seem to stop.

"Do you like that color best of all?" Montrose asked suddenly.

Ophelia blushed crimson as she noticed the duke reflected in the mirror. He was hovering at the doorway to her bedchamber, rumpled and windblown from his ride. A surge of lust hit her hard and she glanced at the fabric quickly to hide her eyes in case he noticed. Not that he ever had before. She swallowed her nervousness and smiled at him. "I've never seen a fabric of this exact shade before. It's beautiful. Thank you again."

He nodded. "I forgot to mention yesterday that I've engaged a London modiste to come to Sherringford to meet with you. Madam du Clair and her assistant will stay for a month to fashion you an entirely new wardrobe."

Ophelia gaped.

He shrugged. "Can't have those silks butchered by an inexperienced local hand."

"Thank you."

He shrugged her thanks away immediately. "I've asked for tea to be delivered to your sitting room for both of us. Do join me when you have a moment."

And then he was gone. Disappearing from Ophelia's bedchamber door before she could even frame an answer. She should really thank him again for all he'd done for her in the last year or so. He was a good man but very hard to get to know.

Ophelia hurried after him, smoothing a hand over her hair

along the way. She had to face facts. Montrose had been let down by another woman and was in pain.

When she entered the sitting room, Montrose stood with his back to her at a window. His posture was stiff again, and the energy in the room made her skin prickle with alarm. He was not over his disappointment, and she so wanted to help him see that there was still hope he could make the match he wanted.

But she would have to tread carefully when she offered any advice. "You wanted to see me?"

"Yes." He sighed. "I saw what you did this morning to the duchess' chambers in preparation for my marriage."

A few more pillows on the chair and settee, a change of painting hung upon the walls, and a thorough dusting wasn't a lot but it was all she'd felt confident she could alter without consulting him first. "I didn't have your permission, and now—"

"I'm not upset. It was very kind of you to think of it really, considering. Beautifully done. I just wanted to say thank you for your efforts."

"You're very welcome." Perhaps her small attention to sprucing up the duchess' apartment went a little way to repay him for all he'd done for her after all. She limped to a chair. "Please, won't you sit, your grace."

He strode to her, and she tried not to gulp as her insides clenched. Not with nerves, however, but with anticipation for being alone with him and perhaps the touch of his hand on her elbow. "You're wearing your new timepiece," he murmured.

She put her hand over it. "It is utterly charming. Just the thing I needed."

"I'm glad." He sank into a chair set slightly to the side of hers with another weary sigh as he stretched out his long legs.

"You sound tired. Did you not sleep well last night, your grace?"

"Well enough."

He was probably still stewing over that woman—the one who'd disappointed him. The tea tray had already been delivered, so she poured tea for them both, and would have offered the duke his cup, except he reached for it first.

"Did you have a pleasant morning ride?"

"I did."

"It looks like a glorious day to be outside."

"There are clouds on the far horizon," he grumbled.

Despite his tone, she smiled. She saw more of him on rainy days. "Then I'd best stroll the garden closest to the manor before the rain arrives. Would you care to join me?"

He seemed to pause but then shook his head. "Unfortunately, I have work that requires my attention." Montrose drew in a heavy breath, his eyes lowered to his cup. "I suppose you still want to know what went on in London."

Montrose was a proud man, and she understood that he was very upset about the woman who'd rejected him. "I only want to understand," Ophelia murmured, lowering her eyes to her cup, too. "I don't know why any lady would pass up the chance to be your duchess. She should have been honored."

"Oh, she was honored to accept the title," he admitted in a bitter tone. "She just didn't want the man who comes with it."

Ophelia glanced up, hating to hear him sound so cast down. "Nonsense."

He was quiet for a long time. "She said she expected to be courted. She imagined I would try to make her fall in love with me before we wed. When I did not achieve those lofty goals, she ended it."

Ophelia was astonished by his candor but glad for it too. "She expected a lot on such a short acquaintance. She should have known falling in love isn't always a lightning bolt. Most often, affectionate feelings grow over time."

"She wasn't willing to wait. She wanted what you had with my cousin. She wanted to be swept off her feet."

"She was a fool then. To think you could not do that for her was to do you an injustice."

"I was just as impatient," he conceded.

"Perhaps so, but it's the way many matches are made in society, isn't it?" She waited to see his nod before she continued. "If she had given you more time, she'd have all the proof she needed of your good heart and generosity. Why, you've done more for me than you ever needed to. I would have sung your praises had I ever met her."

When he looked away, Ophelia assumed she'd embarrassed him with her praise. He did not like to hear the truth of his own good nature. He was a little gruff around the edges at times. Often, if she was completely honest about it. He did not chatter or charm. Not ever. But once a lady accepted the limitation in his manner, she learned to look for the little things, the unexpected kindnesses he did so well. He had approved many adjustments at Sherringford to accommodate her limited mobility. He'd even given up several rooms so Ophelia never had to attempt the stairs to go to bed each night.

"I only did for you what Paul would have expected."

She did not believe that. Paul had told her at the start of their marriage never to expect anything good to come from her connection to the Duke of Montrose. Paul had done his cousin a vast disservice, in her opinion. "You have been very good to me, and I'm sure the right lady will fall for you. You just have to give people a chance to get to know you like I have."

He looked her way. "Her actions have humiliated me."

"I know, but you can rise above the disappointment," she

promised him. She understood all the things he was not telling her in his current state of distress. The Duke of Montrose and her husband had been vastly different creatures. Where her late husband had been outgoing, Montrose was reserved—almost seeming cold at times. That reserve, mistaken for disinterest and rudeness, tended to set many against him.

People said Montrose didn't care about anyone. Ophelia knew better. He cared more than he wanted to reveal.

But Montrose was not above acting out in spite against an adversary. His father had raised him to distrust others, especially those in his own family and he was ambitious. Her husband had told her stories of Montrose that had made her wary of him when they'd first met. Yet since she'd come to live at Sherringford, since the accident, she'd never feared Montrose would turn on her.

For all that gruff nastiness in his past, she found him a remarkable steady companion. Given her unique perspective and place in his household, she had no doubt Montrose took the comfort of his family very seriously. He just didn't like anyone to assume he would rescue them from their own follies every single time they made a mess of their lives.

Ophelia was firmly of the belief that the woman Montrose eventually married would undoubtedly come to feel very loved.

The duke would simply have to start his search for a wife all over again next season. In the meantime, perhaps, there was a way she could help him understand that when it came to matters of the heart, patience was imperative. He should still have faith there was someone meant for him. He just hadn't met her yet.

"I'd be happy to lend any assistance you might need, so you are better prepared to woo a bride when the next opportunity presents itself."

His scowled dark enough to crack the earth. "What makes you think I want to go through that hell again?"

Ophelia wasn't the least bit afraid of his scowls by now. "You have a duty to marry, and you know it. I am sure, given time and the right circumstances, you will easily find the perfect bride. Your duchess is just waiting to be swept off her feet somewhere. Besides, you'd never let your cousin inherit Sherringford for the lack of a son."

His face darkened even more.

She charged on. "Exactly my point. So, you will need a new bride…and perhaps a little practice with the ladies."

He frowned. "Practice at what? I'm hardly an innocent."

Ophelia blushed. She had, of course, heard of Montrose's sexual escapades from Paul, too. Some of them had been quite scandalous tales. Montrose was an attractive man and quite sure to be pursued by ladies in search of a lover or protector. But he needed a wife, the right lady, to marry and give him an heir. Although it would be somewhat forward to discuss a man's past love affairs, when dealing with Montrose it might be wise to be just as blunt. "And I'm a married woman with a broad mind. You should seduce me."

His face slowly turned an alarming shade of purple.

She stretched forward to clutch his hand. "Montrose? Are you all right?"

He suddenly shook his head. "I don't think I heard that right. Did you just suggest I could seduce you?"

"Oh, I didn't mean—" She shook her head and laughed to hide her slip of the tongue. "I did not mean you would actually seduce *me*, but practice how you *could* with the right woman, so she'd see how easy it would be to fall in love with you." She forced another laugh, but it was too much to expect Montrose to laugh along with her.

Ophelia clearer her throat. Montrose needed someone who

could amuse him better than she ever did. Ophelia would make him see that one day soon. If she pushed at him to open up a little more each day, surely he'd discover where he went wrong last time.

"Women like powerful men who will whisper sweet seductions. But they also like men who were not afraid to go out of their way to look a little smitten, too." He seemed about to protest but she held up her hand. "Now, I can understand your dislike of my suggestion. You are a very private man, I know. I promise what we talk about will go no further than my ears alone. Practice courting me, here in private, and I'm sure that you'll have the kind of wife you want in no time at all."

He studied her a long moment. "Do you think so?"

She nodded enthusiastically because he'd not said no out of hand. "Oh, absolutely. One week with me, and you'll feel like a new man, ready to face the marriage market again."

And then he would leave again, embark on another search and perhaps be successful a second time. The thought depressed her.

"What if it doesn't work? What if I really am unlovable?"

"Oh, Montrose. That's simply not true." Montrose was entirely too lovable in her opinion. Sitting alone with him now, she felt herself drawn to him in so many inappropriate ways. But the needs of Sherringford and the family came first. She could not retract her offer. "By the end of the week, you and I will know each other far better than we presently do, and you will discover all is not lost."

His gaze narrowed on her. "I should like to know *you* better before I marry."

Ophelia tried not to feel sad. A wife would forever come between them. She had always known she would lose what little of his attention she had when he married.

Ophelia stole a glance at him only to find him watching her with a question in his remarkable green eyes. Her heart started to thud hard in her chest as the moment stretched. Yes, she had wanted to know the duke much better, too, for so long but had never had a good reason to try to coax him into that sort of conversation. Now she had the perfect excuse to discover what his long silences and hard stares really meant. Knowing him better would help her prepare him for another courtship. She lifted her chin. "I should like that."

Chapter Four

Harry perched on the edge of a delicate gilded chair in the east drawing room, late the next evening, far away from the prying eyes and ears of his servants, hoping the damn thing would not break before Ophelia released him.

Across from him, his late cousin's wife talked nonstop about the things he might say to impress a woman.

Although it might not seem that way to anyone else, every syllable she uttered filled Harry with contentment...and tortured him, too. Harry's cousin had married well but hadn't had the funds to look after Ophelia in the style she'd deserved, in his opinion. Paul's death had allowed Harry to step into the role he'd wanted since the moment he had met Ophelia—and fallen hard.

"I agree," he murmured at the right time.

Ophelia smiled, encouragingly, "And?"

Oh, hell. More words were expected. Harry had promised to let her tutor him how to woo a wife, little knowing how painful it would be. He'd always wanted her with an ache that had never gone away, and pretending to say nice things meant for another seemed incredibly pointless.

He should not crave the company of his late cousin's wife this way, and he'd tried to put his longing for her aside some time ago. The accident—his cousin's fault—had brought them together again.

But each time he saw Ophelia, it was like the first time

they'd met. She rendered him nearly speechless without trying.

He wondered, not for the first time, if he was a fool. Ophelia obviously had no idea how he felt about her. And he'd not the subtlety to hint at it. She thought him a generous family member, a benevolent benefactor, offering the charity of his support as he did with other dependent relations.

He hadn't been charitable; he'd been utterly selfish. Keeping Ophelia secluded under his roof so he might know where she was at all times served *him* more than her. He allowed her to fulfill the duties of the lady of the house because it kept her from dwelling—on her loss of both husband and her missing foot.

Not that Harry cared that she walked with a limp, or continually attempted to hide her impairment from his view. He understood her physical limitations very well by now. He had ordered his servants to keep watch over her at all times— no matter what she said to the contrary.

"I quite agree. The rose vines on the east of the house do need cutting back. I'll have the gardener attend to it at once."

He didn't care about the rose vines. They could smother the house for all he cared. What mattered was that Ophelia was happy and doing well. He still had nightmares over how close he'd come to losing her.

Of course, he'd never actually *had* Ophelia, which was half his problem. He couldn't stop wanting her. He'd gone so far as to flee to London to find a bride so he could avoid ruining everything between them. The damn woman he'd chosen to be his duchess had changed her mind, giving him his marching orders quite rudely, too, at nearly the last moment.

Now he was back, and faced with the worst sort of torture and temptation he'd ever endured.

Seeing Ophelia walking to the carriage with the vicar had put him in a right state, and then the damn fool had tripped her up just so he could pull her close! He'd love nothing more than to send Drayton packing from that living and to put an old man with a wife in his place. Drayton influenced Ophelia far too much for Harry's comfort. But he was thankful the mincing old fool could have less a chance to win this woman's affection than Harry did.

Ophelia could never love either of them. Neither one of them were anything at all like the gregarious cousin she'd married and lost. Paul Shaw, with his infectious laugh, high spirits, and love of adventure, had undoubtedly been the center of her world.

The number of times she'd called out for Paul during her fevers had made him heartsore.

"I had a letter from Mr. Shaw this afternoon," she announced suddenly.

Harry narrowed his eyes. One male living cousin could be found in Brighton, and he was a constant source of annoyance for Harry. "What did Nigel ask for this time?"

"Oh, nothing. Mr. Shaw wrote to say he has married."

Harry rocked back on two legs of his chair, forgetting his manners and his present company. "Shaw couldn't possibly be married?"

"Indeed, he is. To the former Miss Whitcombe, also of Brighton."

An ominous creak had Harry carefully righting his chair before it collapsed beneath him. "She must be barking mad to take him on."

Ophelia clucked her tongue in disapproval of his criticism. He bit *his* tongue over saying more against his cousin or the woman.

"Miss Whitcombe is lovely, sweet, and kind, quite intelligent."

"Intelligent? At least one of them can claim to have that distinction," he mused out loud. Nigel drove him to distraction. He'd been forever getting into one scrape after another when he was younger that, after he'd inherited, had cost Harry money or time to sort out. Harry had sent him to live at a Brighton property he owned, so Nigel might finally learn to fend for himself or perish in the attempt.

The latter had not happened so far. Ophelia had become his champion.

He looked at Ophelia closely now. She was obviously all for the match. "You have met her?"

"Oh, yes. Paul took me to Brighton the first year we were married, and that's where I first met Mr. Shaw, and also Miss Whitcombe, too. We had dinner with her parents and brother, and they are quite a worthy connection for the Duke of Montrose's relation." She cast a quick peek at him, and a gentle smile curved her lips. "I noticed even then that he favored her. I am surprised it took him so long to propose, but then again, we are discussing Nigel Shaw. I suppose her father might not have thought him clever enough to support a wife, despite his connection to you."

So had Harry. "Cousin Nigel has yet to inform me that he's married."

"I'm sure he will." She looked slightly uncomfortable. "Perhaps his letter is still waiting to be opened."

Nigel had probably not written to him yet. He was likely expecting Ophelia to soften Harry up to the idea before he wrote to ask for additional funds. Both Mr. Shaw in Brighton, and Mrs. James, a female relation living in Wales, had written to Ophelia regularly since her arrival at Sherringford. They liked Ophelia more than they did him, even if he supported them all quite generously.

Harry liked Ophelia the best, too.

He crossed one leg over the other, striving to appear comfortable, at ease. In truth, he was starting to become aroused due to their prolonged proximity. Ophelia always had an effect on his libido. Usually he kept their conversations as brief as possible, so he didn't start undressing her in his mind —and then, God forbid, with his hands.

If he offended her by revealing his interest, he might drive her away. That was the last thing he ever wanted to do.

"Your grace," she called.

Harry lifted his attention to her face, chagrined his thoughts had strayed to the impossible pleasure of being intimate with her in any way. His cock twitched when she licked her lips.

He couldn't stay any longer. "Forgive me, I must go and search for that letter."

Her smile was quick, encouraging. "Of course, we can begin again tomorrow. Perhaps at ten o'clock. Here again."

He nodded and stood, quickly turning away before she could notice the thickening at his groin. He could bear another hour here tomorrow if he had to. An hour and no more than that, then he would have to flee. Anything to make her feel her opinion was valued.

She seemed quite keen to see him married to someone else, so he would oblige her eventually.

But not straight away. Not this year. Harry would endure these lessons Ophelia insisted he needed. He probably did need them, really. Women tended to find his manners quite lacking, and his conversation too short.

She called out to him before he reached the door. "The best marriages start with mutual appreciation and desire.

Montrose, it was never just your fault that she didn't love you back."

Harry studied the door latch. Ophelia was kind to say that, but she was wrong. He was to blame. Who could love him if Harry secretly loved another? He appreciated and desired Ophelia, but he was all wrong for her. They were very different. She so light and loving. Him dark and unable to tolerate his own emotions.

Ophelia would never admire him the way she had her late husband. He did not have any luck when it came to the ladies. He'd not the looks, the easy charm that women were drawn to.

He hid his disappointment behind a version of the truth that he could freely admit now. "No, and I didn't love her, either. She was pretty, as much as the next woman, I suppose, and she had a large dowry."

"I promise, the right woman will find her way to you."

Since in his mind he'd already found the woman he wanted, Harry simply nodded and let himself out into the dark hall.

This side of the manor had been set aside for Ophelia's personal use. She'd redecorated it with her own needs in mind. Soft, well-padded chairs, footstools and pillows, and no rugs on the floor to trip her up. Even with the bare floors, it was cozier than anywhere else in the mansion, even in the dark. Ophelia spent most of her time here, running his household very capably with the help of his staff.

He stayed far away, choosing to avoid her for the sake of his sanity, and he latched onto any excuse to spend most of his days on the estate grounds.

The mansion was quiet at this time of night, and his footsteps echoed through the unused rooms. He'd once liked the quiet—the peace of living alone. Everything had changed though when he'd brought Ophelia back with him, still to recover. She'd made him feel lonely when they were apart for any length of time. He'd never met anyone with her courage or determination, and as much as he was drawn to her, he did everything he could to keep a distance.

She regularly made him question his actions, his decisions and opinions. And already, in one day since his return, he'd come to see why he should be grateful to have been jilted.

He would never have been happy with Miss Hayes as his wife.

He was on the brink of entering his study when a footman appeared. "A message has come from Mr. Nash, your grace. I placed it in the center of your desk."

He nodded and strode to his study. The contents were short and to the point. The Johnsons had thrown down their tools and run away from their punishment, leaving their sister behind, alone and unprotected. Nash and his wife had taken the girl in for the night, but something would have to be done for her welfare tomorrow.

Nash suggested the girl might prove a good companion for the future Duchess of Montrose, a governess for their future children. Miss Johnson was much too young to fulfill either role yet.

Ophelia had taken an interest in the girl already. She'd want to have a say in the girl's future, and might just like to have him educate the girl to take on such a position at Sherringford.

He had no objection to that, as long as she was less troublesome than her older brothers.

Ophelia would visit the Nashes alone tomorrow, unless Harry made it plain that he intended to go along, too. The vicar could be there also. He imagined them standing close together in the dark, and Drayton offering to escort Ophelia home.

He lifted his head, determined that not happen. He'd accompany her to the Nashes and remain to keep the old fool at a distance.

Had Maggie Nash written to Ophelia, too?

Most likely, but he didn't recall seeing a letter for her in the footman's hand just now.

Harry penned a note to Mr. Nash, promising to call late tomorrow, and to bring Ophelia with him, and sent the footman off with it.

Deciding to inform Ophelia about helping the Johnson girl, Harry headed for Ophelia's rooms again. It was late now but Harry easily found his way through the dark house.

The door to the east drawing room was slightly ajar, and he pushed it open.

He should have knocked.

Ophelia was lying on her back across the settee with her skirts hitched above her knees. She mustn't have realized the door was not properly shut, because if she had, Ophelia wouldn't be doing what she was currently doing.

She was pleasuring herself.

Very vigorously, too.

Harry couldn't breathe, though he found the wits to step back into the dark hall.

But he remembered everything.

Ophelia's eyes were closed as her fingers rubbed through her cunny and then dipped deep inside her sex. Moisture had glistened on her fingertips as she resumed pleasuring herself with astonishing abandon.

He put his hand on the doorknob and gripped it hard…and glanced inside one last time before he intended to close it.

"Harry," she whispered as her back arched. "Please!"

Ophelia had never used his first name, or nickname, that he ever recalled. But he'd also never heard her mention anyone else by that name, either.

Was she thinking of *him*?

Harry found he couldn't move a muscle. He couldn't tear his eyes from Ophelia's beautifully contorted face. Her pink lips parted to sigh and moan, and her fingers remained on her clit as she said his name over and over again. Her cheeks were delightfully flushed, and his cock swelled beyond his control.

This was the real Ophelia, not the poised and polite widow he'd thought he'd come to know.

Ophelia thrashed. Her legs, even the one missing a foot, dug under the end pillows as her hips suddenly arched high into the air, and then she collapsed. She climaxed very quietly, her hand pressing hard across her mouth, muffling any sound.

She became very still, her eyes fixed on the ceiling above her. She lowered her hand slowly and licked her lips. When she struggled into an upright position, Harry drew back out of sight, but he was curious to know what she would do or say next.

He peeked from the shadows. Ophelia had leaned forward and put her hands over her face, but he heard her words very clearly.

"What am I doing, dreaming of him again?"

Again?

Harry could not stop the smile that burst over his face.

She'd thought of him, more than once, fantasied about him making love to her.

But she was ashamed by it...

Yet so was he, sometimes, when he thought of her, too.

Buoyed by the first hope he'd ever allowed himself to feel about Ophelia, he wiped his emotions from his face and squared his shoulders. If he thought of her, and she thought of him, they might finally get somewhere.

Together.

He glanced through the door again to find her sitting precisely as he'd left her the first time. Composed and perfectly ladylike. But he'd seen her another way now…and he would not rest until he did so again.

He knocked and stepped into the room.

Ophelia yelped. "Montrose! Oh, you scared me!"

Even though she seemed entirely composed, her specially made boot for her missing foot lie some distance away still. He picked it up on his way into the room. The news about the Johnson family could wait until tomorrow. He could see no sign of a letter.

"I am very sorry to disturb you," he murmured. "I had a thought. Instead of meeting here, would you like to visit the lake with me tomorrow?"

"The lake? Is something wrong there?"

"No. Nothing is wrong," Harry said very quickly, scrambling for an innocuous reason to take her so far away from everyone. He never had before, so she would think it unusual. If he took her away from Sherringford early enough, the discussion of the fate of the Johnson girl could wait until later that afternoon. "Perhaps we could conduct your next lesson there, where no one can hear us."

"We do need to cover walking conversation," she mused, obviously seeing nothing amiss with his request.

"Excellent," he said quickly before she could change her mind. "We'll leave early, say nine o'clock?"

"Very well," Ophelia agreed, and then seemed uncertain as she glanced around. "May I have that back?"

He looked at the wooden foot in his hand and shook his head. The prosthetic had pained her to put back on in the early days of her recovery. Especially in the evenings, she'd once said. She hadn't complained of pain since his return, but she often went to bed earlier than him. "I'll help you to bed, if you'd like."

He might like to join her there too, now, but he cautioned himself not to rush. He didn't have the best luck when it came to his love life, and Ophelia was the one woman he couldn't fail with.

He moved forward and scooped her up into his arms even as she made a sound of denial. She didn't protest too hard, though, and he hoped he knew why. Harry had toted Ophelia about while she'd been gravely ill, lifting her up when bedding had needed to be changed while she recovered. Helping her in and out of carriages and inns on the way home. His strength had been beneficial to her when she'd been too weary or weak to move herself.

Unfortunately, he'd forgotten how torturous it had been for him to hold her so close.

He carried her through the room, inhaling her perfume and the underlying scent of her arousal on the air.

The bedchamber door was ajar, and he bumped it open with his toe and carried her in. There wasn't a servant in sight, and he stood in the center of the room, holding her for a moment close to his chest, undecided about whether he could ever release her.

"The stool by the bed," she suggested quietly.

Glad of direction, Harry turned for it and gently lowered her down. As he released her, he allowed his fingers to slowly stroke down her spine…and to brush the back of her thighs, too.

Ophelia was a soft, delicate woman.

And he wanted her in the worst way.

He stepped back, turning away. "I'll send our cousin in Brighton a wedding gift tomorrow. Is fifty pounds enough?"

"More than sufficient, Montrose. That is a very kind thing to do," she called out to his back.

Tomorrow, he'd throw himself into learning how to woo a wife. Ophelia would be the unwitting instructor to her own future in that role. He wouldn't rest until she called him Harry to his face. He wouldn't be satisfied until she admitted she might love him back.

Chapter Five

Ophelia hung on to the side of the little cart, still amazed that Montrose had chosen to take her with him on a morning outing. Usually, he poured over journals and accounts from morning till luncheon. After a second daily ride, he issued instructions for those who worked for him until long after she went to bed. That he was not working, or somewhere about the estate on horseback, was unprecedented. He had a routine that he strictly adhered to. One she had learned to live by and even found comforting.

But he'd presented himself with his customary no-nonsense manner in the hall at precisely nine o'clock. He'd placed her in the open carriage himself and drove off from the manor without a single servant accompanying them.

She wasn't sure what had prompted this sudden change in his routine, but she was glad. Montrose worked far too much, in her opinion. He needed to lighten up a little.

Ophelia wouldn't question his reasons for being with her today for fear that he'd change his mind about taking her lessons. She thought she'd made significant progress in getting his agreement. He's lost that defensive edge to his tone when he spoke about London.

And it was pleasant to be more or less alone with him, so far from the hushed atmosphere of their typical days and any lingering servants. Not that their outing was any different really than any other. Montrose was silent as they drove along. But his thigh pressed continuously against hers in the close confines, making her painfully aware that he was male…and that she found him attractive.

Thankfully, that was an awkwardness only *she* felt. Feelings and longings she'd been incapable of turning aside continued. Making love again was a frequent fantasy of hers. But Montrose would never consider taking her to his bed. He didn't think of her that way. To him, she was Paul's widow, grief-stricken till the end of her days, most likely. But she was not grieving any longer. She'd put aside her mourning and wanted to resume a full life. That included intimacy with a passionate gentleman.

When the lake came into view, Montrose surprised her by turning the horse in the wrong direction, heading past it to another distant lake she'd only heard spoken of. The track led through a stand of tall trees and was obviously far less used, because she began to be tossed about a little more than she cared for.

Montrose shot out his hand across her front to steady her and stop her pitching forward, and then he grasped her by the legs, pulling her hard against his side, capably managing the horse one-handed and her with the other. Ophelia began to grow aroused as Montrose held her and they shifted together with the rocking of the carriage. Mortified, she squeezed her thighs a little tighter, hoping she would not embarrass herself by moaning aloud.

The carriage reached a particularly dense growth beside the track, and she stretched out one hand to brush aside the closest branches.

"Be careful," Montrose murmured, and his fingers tightened on her even more. "It closes in for a while yet."

True to his word, the trees closed in, and she had to

wriggle even closer to Montrose to avoid the scratch of branches against her face, close enough to rest her cheek against his shoulder. She breathed the scent of Montrose deep into her lungs and clung to his arm for safety.

For a moment, she remembered what it was like to be married. Touch, intimacy, and a sense of belonging had been hers at any time, and she missed that.

Finally, they stopped, and as Ophelia sat upright, she dragged her thoughts away from her own longings to look about in amazement. She'd never been to this precise spot before. The view was so beautiful, her breath caught.

Ancient willows dotted the fringe of a nearby lake, their long branches trailing to the ground and into the water. The grass was long, thick, as if no cattle had roamed here for some time.

Montrose dismounted, leading the horse and cart to a nearby tree and hitching it there. He turned back to her, his eyes softer than she'd ever seen them before.

He came to her side. "Wait there a moment while I set up our spot."

She twisted to watch him at work, charging up and down the slight incline carrying a chair and an obviously heavy basket. She marveled at his careful placement of a blanket, the low chair, and the picnic basket beside a weeping willow, so they were not just all lumped together. Nothing seemed to have been left to chance.

He returned, his gaze speculative as he walked toward her. Today he wore his customary buff trousers, white shirt, and waistcoat that matched his dark blue coat. Even though there seemed to be nothing different about him, she was more aware of him than she ought to be. Montrose had admirable proportions, and when he lifted her from the carriage as if she weighed nothing, she couldn't help but sigh out loud that his arms were wrapped about her once again.

Montrose scowled. "I didn't mean to keep you waiting in the sun for so long. Forgive me. You'll be more comfortable in the shade."

Ophelia blushed, glad he'd misunderstood the reason behind her sigh. "I was happy to wait, but I should have helped you."

"It's my outing," he insisted as he set her down on the low chair and then shrugged out of his coat. He settled on the blanket beside her, stretching out his long legs as he took in the view of the nearby lake.

There was not a soul to be seen. No signs at all of human structures even. Just a bird wheeling overhead and the soft caress of a warm breeze across her cheek. "I had no idea this part of the estate was so beautiful."

"Have you not been here before?" At the shake of her head, he scowled again. "I should have thought to bring you here long before now."

"You have more important concerns than entertaining me."

"I cannot think of one."

"It was worth the wait," she promised. Her stomach rumbled, and Ophelia gestured to the basket. "May I?"

"Certainly." He moved it a little closer, too, and flipped open the top.

"Oh!" she exclaimed. There was a huge iced cake placed right at the very top. The duke's favorite, in fact. She lifted it out. "I believe this must be for you, your grace."

His lips twitched as he took it from her and set it down between them. "I thought I heard somewhere that you were partial to cake, too."

"I am, but that is a very large cake," she countered.

"You can never have too much of a good thing."

His words made her smile. She happened to agree with that statement. Montrose would not need very many lessons from her if this was how he arranged a picnic only she was to attend. She found his attention to detail charming and could not understand how he'd failed to win that other lady's heart in London.

"Now, what else has Cook packed for us?" she asked. Ophelia unpacked everything, her mouth watering in anticipation of the dishes arrayed between them. Fresh strawberries and currents and salad greens, boiled eggs and cucumbers, sausage, and even pigeon.

Montrose's cook had sent a feast for at least a dozen, rather than two. "Are we expecting anyone else to join us?"

"I didn't invite anyone. Why?"

"If we ate all this, we might never move from this spot again."

"I'm not planning to move for a good long while." He glanced her way, and then his gaze traveled down her body. He pursed his lips a moment. "Few come this far out, so if you want, you could make yourself more comfortable. Remove your boot if you like, too. Feel the wind in your hair. No one will see you but me."

Ophelia was going to refuse until she saw that Montrose was taking his own advice. He began to remove his boots, then loosened his neckcloth as well and rolled up his sleeves.

Ophelia tried not to stare at his newly exposed neck. The last time she'd glimpsed him so undressed was at the height of her illness. His coat, waistcoat, and cravat had been shed. He'd just been a tired man in a crumpled linen shirt, squeezing her hand as she'd suffered and cried.

She remembered he had dark hair on his chest and very

muscular arms. She'd secretly hoped she might see him again that way.

A little embarrassed by her train of thoughts, she looked down at her legs. She wasn't embarrassed that Montrose might see her short leg; it just wasn't necessarily something a lady should do in front of someone she wasn't married to. It was just her leg, though. Not her whole body, which would indeed be scandalous.

She reached for her foot and untied the laces around her ankle. "Do you come here often?"

"Since my father died, yes."

Since the day the responsibilities for the vast estate had become his burden to bear. Poor man. She knew how everyone depended on him.

Ophelia knew little about the late Lord Montrose. Paul had warned her never to mention the man or his wives. Montrose's mother had been the first bride, but she had died when Montrose was very small. The rest of the wives had each failed to deliver up siblings for the current duke. According to Paul, Montrose had lived a secluded and unhappy childhood here alone.

Ophelia removed her special boot and moaned to be free of the restriction. She could almost believe she could still flex her toes of the foot that only she remembered anymore.

Montrose stared at her leg a moment. "Does it hurt you still?"

Ophelia removed her bonnet, too. "Only if I have done too much."

Montrose dug in the picnic basket and set out wine and two glasses. "What were you doing this morning to be walking too much?"

She blushed again. She didn't want to admit to him that

she was walking around her rooms to combat gaining weight because of inactivity. "Nothing in particular."

He handed her wine. "For you."

Their fingers brushed as she took her glass from him, and she shivered. "Thank you."

He lifted his glass toward her, and they touched them together. "To the future."

"Whatever that may be." Ophelia buried her nose in her glass, inhaling, and then sipped. She did enjoy the bounty of Montrose's cellars—both for pleasure and medicinal purposes. There had been many a night not so long ago made pleasant, pain-free, by an overindulgence of the contents of his wine cellar. Thankfully, Montrose had been only too willing to indulge her medicinal requirements. He kept her chambers well stocked with a variety of liquors. "Lovely."

"I had hoped you might like this particular one." He drank then, too, glancing away to enjoy the view in silence.

She studied his profile. He had the straightest, longest eyelashes of any man she'd ever met. They lie thick upon his skin when he closed his eyes. She longed to stretch out and brush her fingers across them, to discover if they were as stiff as his posture often was or soft the way she wished he'd be.

She looked away, noticing his hands had clenched at his sides. They were often like that. Usually right before he left her...

There was something about her presence at Sherringford that set him on edge, though he never hinted at what that might be.

She worried about what she'd done to set him off today. The uncertainty of her future at Sherringford returned to weigh on her mind, too. She needed to know what to do to make her presence more bearable for him. Only he could tell her if she should start thinking about finding another home.

She gulped some more wine, liquid courage, and then looked at him. "I need to ask you something."

"What?"

"If you had returned a married man, what would have become of me?"

His brow furrowed deeply. "What do you mean?"

She worried at her lip a moment before speaking from her heart. "When you brought me here after Paul died, I was not thinking very clearly. I don't remember if we talked about how long I would stay."

"Forever." His answer was immediate. Definite.

He started to graze on a bit of everything from the plates set out, and Ophelia nibbled, too, watching him closely. She still didn't feel convinced he wanted her here.

"What would I have done? Your wife would have wanted to run the household, as is her right. I would have had nothing to do but stare out the windows."

He looked away. "Is your life at Sherringford so unpalatable and dull that you want to go elsewhere?"

"No, that isn't what I meant. But this isn't my home."

"It can be if you want to stay." He sighed. "I am not married yet, and you are free to run the house any way you wish. Nothing has to change," he promised. "Nothing at all."

She believed he meant that, and finally, she felt confident of her place at Sherringford. She would not have to marry Mr. Drayton, or anyone else, if she didn't love them. She didn't have to imagine going away at all or leaving Montrose in that great big house all alone. "Thank you."

He refilled her glass before she was quite ready and then shifted onto his side, facing her. "If you're not going to eat, why don't you stretch out beside me on the blanket and rest?"

The warm day and the wine were very soothing, and the journey had shaken her about a fair bit. She drank more from her glass and smiled ruefully. "I'm half afraid if I do, I'll fall asleep."

He took her glass and set it on the ground beyond them, next to his. "I'll be here to watch over you."

Ophelia was tempted. It wasn't as if anyone could see her, and as he said, this was her home now.

She eased onto the picnic blanket, and Montrose wadded up his coat for her head to rest upon. It was as sweet a gesture as she'd ever seen from him, and it made her smile. "I'm starting to think offering you lessons is a horrible waste of your time, Montrose. You know exactly how to woo a lady."

"Only time will tell if that is true," he admitted, and then a soft laugh escaped him.

Ophelia stared at him in amazement. She hadn't heard Montrose laugh before. It was a good sound to hear from him now, given his recent disappointment and their discussion of her future at Sherringford. It meant a lot to her, and it was proof he really was comfortable with her being around.

"I promise you will be successful next time."

"I hope so." Montrose wriggled around to lie on his side, facing her. "Are you comfortable?"

"Very." She turned her head to look at him, staring straight into his green eyes. He had such nice eyes. "Are you?"

His tongue darted out to wet his lips, and then her breath caught when he lifted a hand to touch her face. Slowly, he slid a strand of her hair across her cheek and tucked it behind her ear. She shivered as he smiled again. "Actually, yes."

Ophelia nearly swooned. Two smiles from him, and she was in grave danger of behaving in a manner he would not care for. Ophelia easily imagined leaning forward to claim a kiss from him, then crawling on top of his big body and making love to him right there beside the lake. It was the perfect spot to conduct a seduction, and she fought the attraction the only way she knew how.

She imaged how awful it would be when he rejected her because she wasn't a complete woman anymore.

That was enough to make her turn onto her back and fix her gaze on the sky above them until her longings faded. The bird flew in lazy circles overhead. It wouldn't fall to earth because the Duke of Montrose smiled at her. It wouldn't fall in love, either.

The way she *had*.

Ophelia put her hand up to her eyes, shading them from the sun as much covering up her shocking thought. If she hadn't been lying down, she might have fainted there and then. She forced her eyes open, focusing on the bird in a bid to ignore her discovery. "What sort of bird is that?"

"I've not the faintest idea," he murmured.

The tone of his voice was softer, more intimate than she'd ever heard before. It did funny things to her insides yet again.

Ophelia remembered when she met Paul. She had been a little silly about him, trying to catch his notice. She'd known she had to be near him. She felt that way about Montrose now, and not only today.

She stole a glance in his direction. Montrose wasn't watching her anymore. He seemed more interested in the bird, now. "I fear that creature intends to claim the contents of our picnic basket."

Ophelia sat up quickly and handed his grace a plate. "We should make a proper start on lunch so it doesn't go to waste."

The duke sat up slowly, taking the plate from her, but his eyes were full of questions.

She looked at the expanse of water and spoke before he could voice them. "Paul said he swam here as a boy."

"Once. We both did, only I got into trouble for it."

Her cheeks were still hot, and she studied only the expanse of water rather than the man she loved. But she *shouldn't* be in love with him. He'd never want her. "Weren't you allowed to swim here?"

"I wasn't allowed to swim anywhere. Swimming was considered too dangerous. My father had all sorts of rules for what his only son was allowed to do."

Montrose had been an only child. Ophelia had been, too, and she'd had to teach herself a great many things that other children learned from their siblings. "But you swam anyway?"

Montrose dropped a piece of cake onto her empty plate. "Paul taught me that last summer he was allowed to visit Sherringford."

"He taught me, too. Right after our marriage, we stayed a month by the sea. I was nervous about it, but he convinced me to try it. Said it was a wonderful exercise, and I came to enjoy it very much."

Ophelia could feel Montrose's eyes on her, and she forced herself to eat even though she was becoming flustered by him. *By Harry*. The cake was probably wonderful, but her mouth was now too dry to appreciate the flavors.

Montrose passed her glass of wine into her hand. "Do you still swim?"

"What now? No. Of course not." She drank a hasty mouthful of her wine. "I'd probably sink like a stone and drown now."

"I wouldn't let you," he insisted, as if the matter was settled. "I'd be there in the water with you."

Ophelia couldn't help but smile at his continued confidence in his abilities. She wished she had that herself. She stole another glance at him.

Harry clearly had no idea he had her head in a spin, that

her body was begging for his touch. If they were to go on together in the same house, Ophelia had better bury these new feelings deep down, before he noticed. She was supposed to help him find a bride, not keep him for herself.

She finished her cake, mulling over Montrose and what he'd said about his childhood. She could hardly imagine him as a child. But she'd heard Paul describe the late Duke of Montrose. Joyless. Inflexible. Montrose had said he'd gotten into trouble for swimming with Paul, but hadn't elaborated. "What punishment did you and Paul suffer for breaking the rules?"

"Paul was banished, never allowed to visit again."

"And you?"

"The usual."

The way he said "usual" made her heart skip a beat. Punishments should never be *usual*. "Was it so awful you cannot speak of it even now?"

He sighed heavily. "My father's favorite punishment never harmed me. Not physically. He wouldn't endanger his only son's life. He punished others instead. His wives and the servants bore the brunt of his wrath. He kept me at his side and made me watch everything, pointing out it was because of *me* that they were being punished.

"If I showed any signs of concern for their welfare, servants were dismissed. He sent his third wife, a kind woman who had wanted to mother me, back to her parents and annulled their marriage—citing infidelity to shame her, instead of admitting to jealousy. Maggie Nash was once a kitchen maid at Sherringford, too. She was dismissed because she made me laugh. My father saw, and he couldn't stand the idea I might be content."

"That's monstrous!"

"Yes, he was." He shrugged. "Paul knew what my life was

like, what my father did to others, and he still encouraged me to rebel."

"And the only punishment he got was to be sent away."

"It was probably a kindness," Montrose said with a nod. "He had freedoms I never knew."

Ophelia felt sick to her stomach for the injustice of that. Paul had always been good at getting people to do what he wanted. He'd convinced Ophelia to elope after a short acquaintance, claiming to be madly in love with her. Later, he engaged in all sorts of ridiculous and often dangerous wagers with his friends. He'd lived life to the fullest extent, and probably would have continued in that vein even now, if he was still alive.

Harry was the victim of a cold father and her husband's flighty nature. Was it any wonder he doubted his chances of being loved? "What loneliness you must have suffered. Forced to keep everyone you might have cared for at arm's length."

"It hardly matters now, does it?" He pointed at the lake. "I chose to rebel. I chose to swim that day, knowing something would be done about Paul. Being sent away was the kindest punishment my father could inflict on anyone. I could have stayed home in my chambers, or at my studies like I was supposed to do. A dutiful son."

"There's more to life than duty, Montrose. You were just a child."

"I know." He smiled quickly. "I hadn't thought about any of it in years. These lessons of yours have stirred up old memories best left in the past."

Ophelia couldn't forget so easily. So many things about the duke made perfect sense now. She was appalled at how hard Harry's life must have been. His nature might have been so different if he'd been more loved. She wanted to put her arms about him and promise that no one would ever hurt him again.

And that woman he'd almost married had wounded him, too. That made her angry. It made her want to keep all other women at bay. But that was impossible.

Montrose needed a perfect wife, and by God, he would have the right one.

Chapter Six

Nothing had gone right after that perfect, brief interlude looking up at a cloudless sky with Ophelia lying at his side. Ophelia had put her boot back on suddenly, eaten her lunch in near silence, and then shuffled back to the carriage before he was truly ready to return to Sherringford. He'd packed up the luncheon things in a state of bewilderment and hurried to help her into the carriage before she tried to do it herself.

He had done, said, something wrong.

He always seemed to put his foot in it no matter how hard he tried not to with her. He'd shared too much, too soon, perhaps. He'd best remember that women didn't like to hear uncomfortable truths about their deceased husbands, either. Paul had been reckless, a fickle companion.

That day by the lake, Paul had vanished into the trees and returned to the manor without the duke knowing of his involvement in Harry's escapade. Harry had been caught alone—and had sworn he'd been at the lake on his own— intending that Paul be spared any harm. Paul had been sent away that very night, probably suspected of leading Harry astray, because they'd not met again until Harry had assumed the title.

When they *had* met again, Paul had reminded Harry of their adventure to the lake as if it had been a great lark.

Like all the other cousins, he'd had his hand out, too.

Harry hadn't minded supporting Paul so much after

meeting Ophelia. He'd even increased Paul's income from that year onward.

The carriage ride back seemed full of uncomfortable silences. Ophelia refused to engage him in any sort of lengthy conversation, aside from matters that pertained to the management of their home. And once back at the manor, Ophelia had scurried off and disappeared into her room, claiming to have much to do now she had his blessing to stay forever.

Harry resented the assurance he'd given her today. He hadn't meant for her to rush back to her work the way she had.

But she was like him in that respect. She was quite particular about their home. He'd noticed that many times before.

As he glared at the door she'd left through, he cursed himself for making assumptions that the right setting would be easier to reveal his interest in her. She only cared to know she had a future here.

But she had said his name while she'd pleasured herself…

It made no sense.

Perhaps she hadn't meant him, after all. Maybe she dreamed of another Harry as her lover.

He gritted his teeth at the idea of her lying in another man's bed. No. She belonged here, with him. Even if he couldn't have her affection, her body in his bed eventually, she had him. Completely.

Their lessons were over.

He turned away, heading back to his study and the work he'd neglected that day.

He had loved his cousin Paul but had resented him, too. For behaving in a manner that put Ophelia's life in danger. Harry believed the carriage accident had occurred because his cousin was in yet another damn rush to show off and break the rules.

Perhaps that was Harry's problem as well. Was his lack of progress with her merely a case of wanting Ophelia too much, of rushing to change their relationship to a more intimate footing too quickly? He'd rushed proposing to Miss Hayes in London. He would be wise not to do that again with Ophelia.

Unfortunately, Harry was not a very patient man. Once he made up his mind, he tended to think of nothing else but achieving his goal.

Harry looked around his empty office with displeasure. There was so much he needed to do that day, but he could not woo Ophelia even slowly if she was always on the other side of the manor from him. He glanced down at his papers, knowing he must resume working on them. He'd much to catch up on after being away in London.

He sat down and worked until the dinner hour. He did not usually dine with Ophelia more than once a week when he was home. She would not expect him to join her tonight. A pair of servants slipped into the room at seven and deposited a meal for one on a table by the window. Harry studied the single place setting sourly. When the servants were gone, he went back to his work.

Despite his father's adherence to rules, the estate had been a mess when Harry had inherited, and the demands on his pocketbook enormous at that time.

His father had left matters of the estate to indifferent managers. He'd not neglected his two last wives, though, or his mistresses. He'd spent lavishly on them, jewels, homes, his time. Nearly bankrupting his estate. His mother, God rest her soul, had been dead the better part of his life, and he was glad she'd escaped.

Harry had worked tirelessly to turn things around. He had kept his disappointments to himself, not even confessing to his cousin Paul the depths of his disgust with the man whose likeness he bore. He couldn't bear to look at his own face in mirrors more than he had to.

Everyone had assumed Harry was like his father. For a time, he'd tried to live up to the old man's scandalous reputation—even going so far as to boast of his amorous conquests.

He'd taken a few lovers but discarded all of them so very easily. None had filled the void of dissatisfaction in his soul. Only meeting Ophelia had brought light to his life. And even then, she'd been married to his troublesome cousin, a complication that had made him endlessly ashamed.

He'd never doubted avoiding Ophelia was the right course of action. But did she ever crave his companionship at the end of the day?

He rang for a servant to clear the plates away once he'd eaten. "There's nothing more I'll need tonight."

"Very good, your grace," a footman said as he worked. "Mrs. Shaw has returned."

He stilled. "I wasn't aware she had gone out?"

"To visit Mrs. Nash, to discuss Miss Johnson, I believe."

So, there *had* been a letter sent to her. He couldn't help but be curious what Ophelia's help with the Johnson girl was going to cost him. He should have gone with her, too.

He turned back to his desk and his papers. The work went on forever, but he wanted to see Ophelia again tonight and discuss her visit to the Nashes. He'd have to write down what had been decided, and what his involvement might amount to.

Harry collected his papers, folio, pen, and inkpot, and carried everything he might need toward Ophelia's side of the manor. She had a table in her sitting room, and although it would seem unusual, he might make his notes and then finish his work there tonight. Perhaps he could voice his concerns for her safety, if she intended to make a habit of visiting their neighbors after the sun had set.

He passed no servant on the way and tapped on her door, and upon her call to enter, he stepped inside.

Ophelia was standing at her window, gazing on the moonlit garden. She wore a worried expression when she turned. "Montrose. I was just thinking of you."

"I heard you've been to visit Mr. and Mrs. Nash. I assume about the Johnson girl."

"That's correct." Ophelia smiled quickly. "She's a little upset that her brothers have abandoned her. But she's in good hands with Mrs. Nash."

Maggie Nash would mother the Johnson girl until she likely couldn't stand the fussing. "So, she'll stay there?"

"Until after Christmas, I expect. She has an aunt, a woman of considerable means, who might take her in. Mr. Nash wrote a letter to her tonight, but it might take some time to hear back."

"Well, that's good news then."

"Indeed. A girl is much better off with an aunt than going into service as a companion."

"Nash mentioned that possibility to me, too."

"When?"

"In his letter."

She squinted at him. "How funny that Mr. Nash never mentioned writing to you."

"Well, it seems you beat me to taking any action, so it's all turned out for the best."

"Indeed. There's now only the matter of repair to the Johnson cottage and the leasing to a new tenant."

"Well, I cannot do anything about it tonight."

"No, indeed."

Harry lingered, unwilling to leave, now that he'd come.

"Was there something else, your grace?"

"For me, nothing but the desire for a little company." He moved quickly to the oval table before he saw her reaction. "Did you rest enough after your busy day?"

"Yes. Why do you ask?"

He really was terrible at small talk. "I just wanted to know that you were taking good care of yourself. It's not necessary to rush all over the country in the dead of night."

"It's only a little after nine, and I am well, your grace. I would not be standing up if my leg was giving me any trouble. I was just admiring the moonlit gardens."

Was she thinking them romantic? He hoped so. "Do you ever find the manor too quiet at night?"

"At first I did, but I'm used to the solitude now. It's very peaceful here. I'm happy to have company, though. Please do make yourself at home."

He sat down, spread out his work, and bent his head over the papers. He was aware of Ophelia moving around behind his back and lifted his head. "You had a more exciting life before you came to live at Sherringford."

"We traveled a great deal, but I wouldn't say it was all that exciting."

"What would you call it then?" Immediately, he realized he shouldn't have asked that question. "Forgive me. I spoke without thought for your grief."

"You can ask me anything, of course," she promised. "It wasn't a perfect life, I suppose, but I was happy then."

Did that mean she was unhappy now? He had to know.

"What did I do or say during our picnic that was so wrong? I thought you were enjoying yourself, and then you were not. I didn't mean to upset you with talk of my childhood."

"Nothing you did or said was wrong."

"You are not being honest with me," he said, shaking his head. "I wish Paul had been with us today, instead of me alone. Did you hate to learn that he wasn't always the perfect hero of your memory?"

He worked while he awaited her answer.

"No one is perfect," she whispered.

"It is all right. I know we are nothing much alike. He meant a lot to you, and of course you would rather I'd been him."

A shaky breath left her lips. "I haven't thought of Paul very much in a long time. I don't miss him the way that I used to."

"Then what is it?" He drummed his fingers on the desk as she paced behind him. "You said I hardly needed lessons in wooing a lady, but the next moment you became cold toward me."

"You will do well when you go back to London to look for a wife."

"And if I don't go back to London?"

"But you must if you are to meet a suitable lady to marry."

He couldn't hold in the truth any longer. He had to know if she might ever look upon him with any favor.

"Must I, Ophelia? You know my limitations when it comes to courting and polite conversation. People don't like me, or if they say they do, they're only pretending until my back is turned. Tell me what I must do better?"

"Nothing." There was a sigh and a step behind him. "I never lied to you. Any woman would be happy to be courted by you."

"But you don't want me to court *you*?"

"Montrose," she chided. There were a few minutes of silence before she spoke again. "You cannot be serious."

"I have never been more so. There is no one better suited

to run this household than you. I thought for a while that the things other women dislike about me did not offend you as much," he told her. He signed a letter and set it aside. "I went to London not looking for love, but to marry a woman I could tolerate in my bed. Most nights, I imagine *you* there."

"What!"

Harry cringed at her outcry. "It is not something I'm proud of."

"I cannot imagine…"

He sighed. So, he was alone in his admiration. The disappointment was crushing. He'd never met a woman who appealed to him as much as Ophelia always had.

"I'm sure Paul whispered in your ear about me, told you things about my past behavior that you find unpalatable. Before my father died, I was an angry young man. When I first became duke, I grew worse. I was determined to earn my reputation in the world. I wanted to be considered formidable beyond the borders of the Sherringford estate. A man no one could refuse or cross, no matter whom it hurt. Those enemies to this day still get under my skin. My time in London was not well spent. I wish I had stayed here with you."

"Everyone has something in their life they regret. Even Paul had flaws," she answered.

"He had the good fortune to marry you." Harry shook his head. "He had everything."

"He was not faithful to me," she said in a whisper.

Harry whipped around to stare at her, completely stunned. "That's not possible."

She shrugged, her face flaming. "I saw them myself."

Harry could not fathom why Paul had strayed from this beautiful woman's side for even a moment. "I had no idea. I'm sorry."

"It wasn't your doing." She raised her chin, defiant and

determined not to let the humiliation get the better of her. "He didn't even realize that I knew about them."

"Fool." There was still more he wanted to say, but he'd always had trouble speaking of things that really mattered to him. He loved her but he was afraid. Perhaps if he didn't look at her directly, he might be able to get the words that filled his heart out at last. Harry quickly turned back around and wet his lips before speaking. "You are my cousin's widow. And…I should not imagine making love to you. But I cannot stop."

Ophelia made no replay, and after several minutes of strained silence he realized he'd said far too much.

He started to gather up his papers. "Of course, I can understand you might be distressed by my confession, how could you not be. I will understand if you wish me to leave you be. The last thing I have ever wanted was to upset you. So, if you would prefer to live elsewhere now, I can offer you a choice of several homes. Near one of my cousins, if that will please you. You will have everything you could ever need for your comfort; I promise. Servants, money. Anything."

He heard her move to stand behind him. "Do you really imagine me in your bed?" she asked quietly.

"Quite often." He saw no point now in denying his base impulses anymore. He had nothing left to lose. "I think if I had met you before Paul did, I would have made you my duchess. You would have never lost your foot and endured such agony then, and challenges now. I care about you, Ophelia. I thought we could be good together. And I would do anything to make you happy…even lose you."

He began to write out a refusal to attend a house party in Wales this winter when Ophelia softly settled her hands on his shoulders. He instantly leaned back into her touch, his heart beating hard against his ribs. It was so rare that anyone touched him, and that she had reached for him now gave him some small sense of peace.

She squeezed his shoulders. "You do know how to say all the right things, Harry."

Her lips suddenly pressed against the stubble of his night beard. A soft kiss that made him gasp out loud.

"I dream of you, too," she whispered.

That admission was all he needed to hear.

Harry spun around, pulled Ophelia onto his lap, and stared at her pink cheeks, parted lips, and bright eyes.

She reached for his face, and he flinched away, expecting a slap.

But all she did was cup his cheeks and hold him steady. "I won't ever hurt you," she promised. "Close your eyes."

"Why?"

"Just humor me for a moment. Go on. Close them."

Although he felt somewhat foolish, he closed his eyes to the vision sitting on his lap. Ophelia traced the contours of his face with her fingertips...and then softly brushed his eyelashes. When she sighed, he opened his eyes and found her still studying him from inches away. God, her eyes were worth drowning in.

She moved closer, lips parting, and then stretched the rest of the way to claim his own.

Finally.

Harry framed her face with his hands and parted her lips with his tongue. Hers darted out to tangle with his almost immediately, and he was utterly lost.

She tasted of wine and sweetness. All the things Harry was not, and never would be. She was still too good for him, but she'd chosen him. He'd never endanger a heart so precious.

Her fingers threaded through his hair at the nape, and he

became aroused by the feminine warmth pressing against his body. He would be hers in every way. He'd never betray her the way her first husband had. He'd love her until the end of time.

Harry kept his eyes open as he kissed her again and again, unwilling to miss a single moment of such exquisite happiness.

Chapter Seven

Ophelia had thought it a cruel twist of fate that she was attracted to the duke. But the Duke of Montrose was kissing her as if he couldn't get enough. For a moment, she forgot where she ended and the usually stern duke began.

Harry, the object of her erotic dreams, desired *her*. His expectation of rejection had cut her to the quick and almost had her in tears. It seemed unbelievable that he harbored such doubts about himself, and yet she could feel the desperation in his kiss.

Only time would reassure him—and she would start tonight. She had no power to resist the man, now that she knew he truly felt the same about her. His hands traveled over her body restlessly, lightly, making her feel so wonderful and cherished. Being in his arms like this was better than she had ever dreamed it might be.

She wrapped her arms about his shoulders and gave herself over to passion completely. She kissed him back, tangling her tongue with his and devouring his mouth with a hundred searing kisses. She could not get close enough to the man she would openly admit she unabashedly adored.

She wasn't going to let Harry escape her tonight, either. Ophelia was not ashamed she enjoyed pleasure and making love. She wanted the duke in her bed.

Tonight.

Her husband had once complained that her insatiable

hunger for intimacy taxed his strength. The lack of pleasure in their marriage bed after the first few years had been a source of friction between them until the day Paul had died. Even before he'd been unfaithful, she'd known loneliness in the marriage bed.

She suspected now that there had been other women in his life all along. But his last woman had been special to him. She'd lived on the opposite side of their small town. Because of her influence, Paul had finally turned away from sharing any intimacies with Ophelia at all.

Ophelia hadn't been touched by any man but her husband. She desperately hoped that Harry was different when it came to passion.

If Harry had wanted her all these years, and believed her indifferent to him, she could understand why he always seemed irritated. But he had no reason to be that way anymore. She was quite ready to have him take his frustrations out on her in the bedchamber.

Ophelia cupped his face again, teasing her tongue into his mouth until he moaned.

Harry broke the kiss. "I want to fuck you."

"Yes," she whispered, though her cheeks warmed at his bold language. Being his lover was what she wanted. She was already halfway gone in desire, and all he'd done was kiss her, touch her. She'd likely come the moment he entered her, she was that aroused. His roving hands and kisses made her pussy quiver.

She tackled his cravat, pulling the fine material away from his throat. Harry began to tug at her bodice, drawing the material down off her shoulders so he could pepper them with kisses, too.

She wanted more than that, and since her gown seemed

loose enough, she wriggled her shoulders to bare her breasts. When a nipple was revealed, Harry quickly kissed it and then took the peak into his mouth. She sighed with pleasure as he suckled her expertly. He was rougher than Paul, hungrier, and that suited her needs tonight.

Ophelia tangled her fingers into his hair and held him firmly pressed to her breast. She was not afraid to direct a duke's lovemaking. She knew what she liked and what wasn't enough to satisfy her.

When Harry lifted his head at last, she pressed her lips to his throat and nipped at him. She kissed and nibbled the strong column and then caught the lobe of his ear between her teeth. She bit lightly as he gasped out loud again.

Harry's hot hands slid around her back, playing with the laces of her stays, loosening her garments further, and then he captured both her breasts in his big hands. She sat back as he played with her nipples until they became hard points, and ached. She squirmed on his lap as her sex quivered again. "I want you to touch me everywhere."

"You'll feel me inside you soon enough," Harry threatened.

He stood, and then they were moving toward her bedchamber, Ophelia held firm in his arms. She so hoped for an energetic tumble and a great deal of satisfaction for both of them.

Harry lay her on her back, gently lifted her skirts to her knees, and then arranged her body how he wanted her. He caught her legs at the knees and slid her gown higher up to her thighs.

The look on his face suggested he was enjoying himself, though he didn't smile. He brought his lips to her knee, and she looked down upon his dark head as he kissed her sensitive skin. But then he surprised her completely by removing her slipper, her wooden foot and then her stockings…to kiss the very end of her shortened leg over and over.

She blinked away tears as he continued, astonished and grateful that he was not repulsed by the ugly scars.

Eventually, he moved on to kiss the rest of her in that exact same fashion, worshiping both her legs with soft kisses, rising slowly toward her aching sex.

He lifted her gown higher still and placed one soft kiss directly on her curls. He widened her legs and inhaled, and then his fingers teased into her folds. "You're wet."

Ophelia squirmed, eager to feel him inside her soon. "You're an exciting man."

"I haven't been this hard in a long time," he admitted.

She glanced down his body to see the proof of it straining at his groin. When he suddenly slid his fingers inside her, Ophelia squeezed her eyes shut and barely held off her orgasm.

Harry brought his head close to hers, but his fingers continued to slide deeper into her. "Do you like the way I touch you?"

"Yes," she whispered, then met his gaze. She'd never seen his expression more severe than it was tonight. His focus on her body drew her to him, increased her pleasure. Ophelia widened her legs a touch more and tilted her hips. "I can take more."

He grunted, and then he obliged her by sliding more of his fingers inside. She was stretched wide and close to coming apart, but she loved the feel of him. The ache only intensified when he took her nipple back into his mouth again while he fingered her. She didn't want it to be over too soon, but she ground down on his hand, courting the fine line of pleasure and pain.

Harry released her breast, and suddenly his tongue was lapping at her clitoris. She bucked against his face and fingers, desperate now to come. She was on a path that led directly to pleasure without stopping. When he sucked her clit hard, Ophelia came and came and came.

She slowly opened her eyes after she'd regained her senses. Harry was kneeling between her spread thighs now, watching her face, his fingers still wedged inside her, his lips damp from kissing her sex.

He carefully removed his fingers, but only to rub her dampness over her sensitive pussy. When he parted her folds, leaned down, and blew lightly over her sex, Ophelia was rocked by another tightening of her inner muscles. "Harry!"

"I have you," he promised. There was a decidedly large bulge pointing toward her from his breeches. She watched him curious to know when he would take off everything that separated them. He seemed in no rush, though she was aware of his hunger.

He removed his upper garments with painfully slow movements, watching her through hooded eyes. A slight smile turned up his lips but he said nothing as he continued to torment her with his slow strip. As his shirt hit the floor, Ophelia groaned.

Harry was big all over, hard-muscled and taut-skinned. The dark hair she'd glimpsed at his throat continued down in a line to his groin. She stared at the buttons on his breeches, and then lifted her head as he continued to unbutton himself in his slow fashion.

And then he moved his hands aside so she could see.

Her cunny gave a surprisingly enthusiastic twitch at her first peek at his impressive cock springing from his loosened breeches. She would feel very stretched when he was deep inside her. She'd never had a cock that big, but she wasn't afraid. Not of Harry.

He would take care of her.

He always had.

Harry shoved his breeches further down his thighs and wrapped his hand around his cock at the base. He stroked himself, and his lips twitched. "Do you think you can take this easily?"

Ophelia widened her legs and tilted her cunny up. "Not easily at first, but willingly. Come to me."

"Not yet," he said as he lowered his hand between her legs again.

When he slapped her there, she gasped from the unexpected pleasure. "Oh!" she cried. "That felt so strange."

"Good strange?"

"Yes, Harry. Very good. May I have another?"

He growled and did it again. Then he grabbed one of her hands and forced it between her legs. "Open yourself to me."

Moisture gushed from her sex at his bold demand, and she did as he asked very eagerly, playing with her sex a little, too —the way she'd only done when alone.

Harry leaned down for a close-up view of her cunny. After a moment, he looked up along the length of her body, and he finally smiled. "You've a pretty thatch, Ophelia. I'm going to take great pleasure in sliding my cock into you all night long."

Ophelia quivered both from his use of her first name and from his intentions. His coarse way of speaking might have offended another lady, but she suspected Harry was finally being himself, in a way he'd never dared before. She liked this side of him. He was exciting, and she found his coarseness arousing. She hoped he meant it, too. Ophelia had never been entirely satisfied with making love but once in a night.

She pinched her lower lips hard, pulling them wider, but

then reached for Harry's cock instead. He was thick and hot against her palms, and he moved closer so she could fondle him without stretching. Using both hands, she stroked him over and over, bringing her thumbs up over the ruddy head and back down again to the base. She made him moan when she spread his moisture around the tip and then licked some from her fingers.

Although she would have willingly taken him into her mouth, she was desperate to feel him inside her cunny. She ached to have Harry come apart the way she had. To give him the pleasure that would sate him. She wanted to make him as happy as he was making her tonight.

She wrapped her fingers around the base of his cock and guided him to join with her.

He was big, but he was careful. He claimed her slowly, even when she begged for more. He never once took his eyes from hers.

And in that moment, she realized what he'd been trying to tell her, show her, in his own strange way since she'd woken with her fingers tangled in his hair. He wanted her as much as she wanted him. They had both been afraid.

When he was fully inside her, but remained still, Ophelia clawed at his back. "Harry! Don't make me wait."

"You belong with me, now and forever." His jaw clenched a moment. "Do you understand? You are mine."

Her pussy clenched around him. She wanted that to be true. "Yes, Harry. I want you just as much, I swear."

He chuckled darkly against her ear. "I doubt that. I want you panting and desperate now, and sated and soft after. I want you tonight. Tomorrow. Until the day I die."

"I need that too," she promised. "Please make love to me."

He drew back his hips and began to thrust into her, slowly at first, and then when she had grown accustomed to his size, he became less gentle. Ophelia encouraged him until he was slamming into her—chanting her name with each thrust.

Ophelia raised her hands to the headboard to steady them. Harry took advantage of her position to claim her nipple and suck hard.

Ophelia came again, and he did, finally, as well.

Harry collapsed atop her in a sweaty tangle of heavy limbs and hard breathing. Ophelia wrapped her arms around his head, her legs about his hips, and thoroughly enjoyed the pleasant weight of him pressed against her.

Being with Harry in her bed was better than any fantasy she'd ever conjured up.

Her cunny pulsed still, squeezing around his softening cock.

She clung to Harry, unable to believe how much he excited her even after all they'd done together. She already knew she wanted more of him tonight, tomorrow, and forever. She wanted everything he promised, and so much more. He hadn't spoken of marriage or love, and she did not assume he ever would.

This was enough for now. For once, finally, they understood each other perfectly.

Harry seemed in no hurry to move off her, so she rocked her hips, making him move inside her again. He was coming along nicely, and then he began flexing his hips into her again, too.

After several pleasant minutes of grinding, he rolled onto his back, dragging her on top of him.

Ophelia struggled into a comfortable position and looked down on his flushed face. She touched his cheek as she continued to rock on his stiffening cock. "You asked what happened today that changed my mood," she whispered. "I thought of what it would be like to have you under me like this."

A slow grin spread across his face. "Then you read my mind, too. I was moments away from attempting to seduce you."

"I would have liked that. We were so alone."

"I'll take you to the lake tomorrow. Strip you bare, open your legs and kiss you till you come on my face. And then I'll drag you atop me like this and let you take me all the way in until you come again."

She bit her lip as he bucked under her, and they began to make love with her on top. Just the way she liked to have *her* Harry. Smiling and handsomely disheveled. He didn't seem to mind that she was setting the pace. He skimmed his fingertips over her skin and seemed content to watch her cunny take him in.

Yet when it came to passion, it did no good if only one partner got to make all the decisions. She pushed his hair from his face and regarded him though narrowed eyes. Harry had a dirty tongue, and she imagined him more adventurous in bed than ever her late husband might have been. There was much he could teach her about passion.

She leaned down, close to his ear to whisper, "Tell me what you desire?"

"You," he promised as he squeezed her bottom firmly.

She grinned. "Would you like me on my knees so you can take me from behind, Harry?"

Harry stilled a moment.

Then with an inarticulate roar before Harry withdrew, flipped Ophelia onto the mattress, onto her belly, and then her knees before she could laugh at his haste.

He sank into her again, and his hands were clamped on her hips, steadying her as he drove into her repeatedly. She gasped as her inner walls tightened and quivered anew as he dominated their lovemaking and made his enthusiasm for the position quite plain.

Ophelia put her fingers to her clitoris and brought herself to orgasm just as he found his second release. It seemed, in the secret dream she'd kept close to her heart for so long, that in Harry, she also might have found her true match in passion.

Chapter Eight

Harry sat up in a strange bedchamber with a start and looked about the dark room in a state of confusion. It took him a moment to remember why he had fallen asleep in Ophelia's bedchamber.

When he remembered the night of passion that had passed, he reached for her, eager to start all over again.

When he didn't find her beside him, he jumped out of bed and threw open the heavy drapes, confused even more that it seemed to be nearly midday. She should be here with him even now. He might have slept longer than he usually would, not surprising given the erotic exertions of the previous night, but this was her room. She should have at least woken him when she'd risen.

Harry had lost count of the number of times and ways he'd made love to Ophelia last night, but he could remember that each and every time, she'd snuggled up to him afterward. She had undoubtedly enjoyed what they'd done together. He'd promised to continue their amorous activities by the lake where they'd picnicked.

He looked about her chambers, saw that his clothes had been laid out neatly for him to find, and he rushed to get dressed before a servant discovered him naked. Once dressed, he snatched up the mantle clock, squinting at it as he confirmed the exact time. Three minutes to noon, and he was lucky that no one had found him here yet.

As he raked his fingers through his hair to straighten it, he wondered how long ago it had been since Ophelia had left him. There were things they needed to discuss today. He was keen to have a date decided for their marriage.

He checked no one was about and slipped out to her sitting room. His papers were all still as he'd left them, and he scooped them up before striding boldly back to the side of the house he'd typically inhabit. From tomorrow, he decided, it would be *their* house: no more sides, no more separations.

The only small matter that gave him pause was the location of the master bedchamber and the number of difficult stairs Ophelia might be required to attempt every morning and night, after spending the night together. She was not particularly agile on stairs, and that had always worried him. He couldn't always be around to carry her down.

He would figure something out; perhaps an inventor he'd heard of recently might devise a way for Ophelia to move about more easily between the floors. Enough money could usually inspire anyone to create something new.

He rushed up to his own chambers, found fresh clothing in his dressing room to put on, and returned below to begin the hunt for the woman he would marry.

It was nearly an hour later when he heard a carriage on the drive, and Ophelia returned with a maid by her side. He hovered just out of sight as the butler took her hat and coat from her in the hall, handed her a letter, and only when the servants were gone did he rush out to confront Ophelia about her disappearance.

She turned as she heard him approach. Her lips parted, and then she swallowed before attempting to curtsy. "Your grace."

"None of that," he warned. He would not have Ophelia attempt curtsies anymore. She might fall. And since he hadn't seen her in hours, he moved closer.

Harry didn't fight against the hardening of his cock or the impulse to touch her. He pulled Ophelia into his arms and looked down upon her upturned face. A blush was slowly climbing her cheeks, and her lips parted on a pant. "You weren't there when I woke up."

"No." She moved away, into a chamber that he'd thought of hers since she'd come to live with him. It was a comfortable room, with a long wide chaise Ophelia often reclined on when she was weary. The chaise was big enough for them to share actually.

He put his hand under her elbow, ready to lead her there to sit and perhaps make love again if she was agreeable.

But she set her reticule on a nearby side table, her brows drawing together in a frown as she glanced his way. "I had something I needed to do in the village."

He shook her gently. "And it couldn't wait until I woke up, and we'd spoken about what happened between us last night?"

Ophelia pulled out of his grip. "No, it could not."

"I would have driven you myself. I told you I would look after you."

"It was because of last night that I had to go alone." She sighed. "There are some things you cannot help me with. Sometimes I will need a moment of privacy to speak with other people, too."

He narrowed his eyes on her, not liking that answer. "Judging by your frown, you spoke with the bloody vicar again. What could you possibly need him for that couldn't wait?"

She stared at him. "Yes, I went to speak with Mr. Drayton. He asked something of me that I needed to give him an answer to. It couldn't wait."

"Another charitable cause? A donation of men and money

to fix another leaking roof? Or was it the parish orphans again?"

"It was nothing like that. It was very personal." She sighed. "While you were away, Mr. Drayton asked me to marry him."

Harry could not have been more shocked. His first instinct was to rush out of the mansion and go down to the village, find the vicar, and punch him right in the nose for presuming himself good enough to ask Ophelia such a question. "Why, that grasping, underhanded—"

"He's nothing of the sort, and you know it. He's a kind man." She shrugged. "I owed him an answer."

Harry didn't want her to feel she owed anyone, least of all the vicar. "I hope you told him to go to hell?"

"I said what was kindest." She turned away. "He was disappointed."

Harry smiled. "He'd better get over it quickly."

"I hope so." She opened her letter, and she then nodded. "Cousin Miriam is increasing again."

"Another brat to murder our ears when it cries," he grumbled. "Wonderful."

Ophelia didn't respond to that.

Harry moved to stand behind Ophelia and set his hands on her shoulders. She was stiff, and did not turn to welcome his attentions. Had he been too demanding in bed last night? He'd imagined their morning quite differently from the way it had turned out so far. More kisses, and a decision about how long she'd make him wait to bed her again. He was under no illusions that Ophelia didn't have an opinion on that.

They ought not to have anticipated their wedding night. There was any number of people in the district who could count the number of months from wedding night till the birth of their first child. He would rather not involve Ophelia in any unsavory gossip if he could help it. She might have a hard time when they returned to London next spring. He would shield her from as much of the unpleasant reception they would get if he could.

He took a steadying breath, eager to begin negotiations for their marriage. Time was passing. "If Drayton carries on, I'll find someone else to marry us."

Her head lifted. "Are we getting married, then?"

Harry blinked, then spun Ophelia around to face him. She regarded him with a great deal of astonishment. Surely she couldn't have thought he'd no honorable intentions when he'd taken her to bed? He frowned. "Of course we are."

"You never asked."

Harry threw up his hands. "I warned you I was no good at this sort of thing."

"A lady likes to be asked," she replied, refolding her letter. "It might seem unnecessary between us now, but I would like to tell our children about this day. And yes, *they* will cry, too, and you cannot be cross about it, either."

"I'll try," he promised, but he liked the idea of a dozen of his own brats running about the estate yelling at each other in a way he'd never been allowed to do. He'd watch from a safe distance with Ophelia, out of harm's way. There would be very few rules for *their* children.

He raised her face to his, and she leaned into his touch. "You're going to need to be a little more obvious about what you want from me if we are going to get along. I wasn't brought up to share my innermost thoughts with anyone."

"You must confide in me. Hold nothing back. I won't try to manipulate you or betray your trust. Hurting you is the last thing I will ever do."

Her words made his eyes sting, but he forced the strong emotions away. He wasn't able yet to be the man she expected. But he would try to change—to meet her halfway if he could. He would try hard.

He sighed. He would have to start today. Nothing less than a grand proposal to make her feel his love would do. He'd already made her doubt her place here, and now his intentions, too. He was probably going to have to make their wedding more of a fuss than he could stand, because she would secretly want that, too.

He squared his shoulders. "You are the last woman I'll ever ask to marry me, so here goes."

He swept her up into his arms and carried her back into the empty front hall. He set her down on her feet carefully, made sure she was steady, and then whistled loudly.

He whistled again, and the servants came at a run.

Good.

He wanted this moment to be as widely reported as possible. "Gather round," he ordered. "Gather round."

Ophelia tugged on his sleeve. "What are you doing?"

"The right thing."

He waited for even the gasping cook to finally arrive. By then, enough had gathered around the room or hovered overhead on the stairs to provide sufficient witnesses.

Then he sank to one knee and held out his hand to Ophelia.

The servants drew in a collective gasp and started to mutter amongst themselves immediately.

Ophelia's eyes filled with tears, and she glanced around at the servants until they fell silent.

Then he drew in a deep breath. "Ophelia Shaw, you would make me the happiest man in all of England if you would consent to be my wife and duchess. Mother of my children, mistress of Sherringford...forever."

Her small hand slipped into his, and she nodded,

dislodging the tears that had turned her eyes glassy bright. "I would be honored."

He pressed ardent kisses to her knuckles, then stood to wipe her tears away from her cheeks with the pads of his thumbs. "I am in love with you," he told her, not caring who heard him speak. Most likely, no one would believe he could love *anyone*. Only Ophelia would need to believe him. Her opinion was the only one that had ever mattered.

"And I love you, too," she promised. "So very much."

The servants start to whisper excitedly, and then one of them started a slow clap. Soon all the servants had joined in and were talking about them making such an unexpected match. It seemed his decision had their approval.

Ophelia held on to his arms as she practically bounced in front of him. "Oh, Harry! You are so full of happy surprises."

"Be careful," he warned, tightening his hold on her in case she overbalanced on her wooden foot.

"That was the most memorable proposal in the history of forever. No one will ever dare claim you're not a romantic man at heart when they hear about this."

He pulled her close and pressed his forehead to hers. "I'm only ever romantic when I think of you. I'll send money to Miriam for the babe, extra for the midwife and wet nurse, too."

"Thank you, Harry." She wrapped her arms tightly about his neck, and he lifted her off her feet. "You are the sweetest, most generous man in the entire world."

Harry held her tight against him, little caring that the servants were still watching him with a mixture of surprise and, likely, horror. Ophelia was popular with the servants. He was decidedly not. He bent close to her ear. "You do realize you are the only person who sees me that way."

She laughed. "Oh, I know I'm the most fortunate of women to have seen your best side."

"*You* are my best side," he countered, nuzzling her neck until a sudden thought occurred to him. He had to lay down some ground rules about their life together. "The cousins are not coming to live with us."

Ophelia wriggled, and he set her on her feet with the same care he'd always shown her. She lifted a hand to his face and smoothed his hair back from his eyes. He closed them, enjoying the caress, then felt the tickle of her touch flutter across his eyelashes again. "Yes, Harry."

"I absolutely forbid it," he said, as he pressed his cheek firmly against her tiny palm. He liked her touching him and considered how easy it might be to lure her to some out-of-the-way corner to talk in greater privacy. Although they could make a decision about their home anywhere or anytime. Even in bed. That thought cheered him immensely. "They'll expect you to entertain them. I want you all to myself."

She pouted a little. "You have me, Harry."

He sighed at the happy thought. They were to marry; they'd made love like lust-crazed fiends. There was no chance she'd jilt him. So what was the harm in offering a compromise now if it made her happy in the long run? He wanted this to be a good marriage for both of them. He was certainly no prize. She undoubtedly would have the chore of smoothing out his rough side and placating people who thought they'd been insulted by him for the rest of their marriage.

"Fine. They can come for the wedding and Christmas, but just this one year. You'll have the sole responsibility for organizing everything. I'll leave everything to you and the servants. I don't want to hear a word about them until they get here."

"Thank you." She laughed again and then played with a

button on his waistcoat. She winkled her adorable little nose. "You'll hardly know they're on the estate, I promise."

He grunted. "I thought that about you once."

Ophelia laughed and turned away. When she requested tea for two in her private apartment and dismissed the servants with a wave of her hand, Ophelia was instantly obeyed. But he couldn't help noticing the servants left smiling rather than rushing off, as they did with him.

At least in choosing her for his duchess, he'd done something right for the good of everyone at Sherringford.

Ophelia beckoned Harry to join her with a cheeky smile that instantly made his cock thicken.

Harry tripped along behind her. A proper courtship would typically involve separations and meetings and chaperones. But they already lived in the same home, more or less alone.

"Shut the door, Harry."

He obliged and then couldn't help but laugh out loud. Ophelia knew more about proper courtships than he ever could. If she didn't trouble herself, observe the rules, damned if he'd even try.

"What's so funny?"

"You. And me." He grinned. "Do you have any idea how I've tortured myself over you?"

"I've some, but Harry, the torture might just be beginning for both of us." She sat herself down, patting the space beside her. "There's a real danger we're going to be interrupted when the tea arrives."

Harry hurried to her side and leaned in to steal a kiss. His hand fell to her knee, and he slid it along her thigh. "Then I'd better make every moment alone with you count."

"We both will," she whispered, caressing the front of his trousers.

He nibbled her neck, and she arched up toward him for

more. She took his hand and placed it on her breast, and he pinched her nipple through the fabric of her gown, eliciting the most erotic moan he'd heard from her yet.

They'd have to stop when the servants came, but even those small inconveniences didn't diminish his current state.

Harry was happy, perhaps for the first time in his whole life. He was free to love Ophelia the way he wanted to. The way he needed to. He didn't have to change himself to be considered lovable.

Ophelia began to slide sideways, drawing him with her until they were both lying down, him atop her. If this was a glimpse of his future, he would happily court Ophelia every day of his life.

She wiggled some more, and he was suddenly wedged between her spread thighs. He raised himself up to stare at her flushed face, lips plump from his kisses. She was already his perfect match, his love, his life, in every way that could ever possibly matter—especially when it came to passion. He wiggled his hips just to hear her moan. "Should I show you my love again, Ophelia?"

Ophelia's answering smile was decidedly wicked. "Always, Harry, and then it's my turn to love you just as much."

Epilogue

Two months later

Harry lifted Ophelia down from the carriage in front of the village church in a terrible temper. There was absolutely no reason for him to attend church services on Sundays, but one reproving glance from his duchess, and he resigned himself to never having another Sunday morning to himself again.

He wouldn't dream of allowing Ophelia to attend without him. The vicar had once had a soft spot for her. No man would come between them if he could help it. So, he found himself following Ophelia to Sunday services, all about the countryside, too, visiting his neighbors, and that was the best part of being a husband, in his opinion. He no longer had an excuse to spend his days alone, and he did not want to go back to the way things had once been, either.

He'd been lonely. Not that he'd ever put a name on what he'd felt before Ophelia had loved him.

Ophelia strode along beside him easily now, since the purchase of a new and properly fitted boot. The new contraption was one of a dozen he'd had made for her, all lined with the softest of sheepskins and far more forgiving padding than she'd ever enjoyed.

They argued. Often. Ophelia no longer simply endured his moods in silence. It was sometimes almost a pleasure to be taken to task for his surliness. Making love after a particularly heated discussion kept them both sated and only ever brought them closer.

He let her lead him into the church and stood back while she greeted the other parishioners. They were not here to speak to him, anyway. Harry had no illusions that marriage to a good woman had made him more popular. She had a mind of her own, and he wanted it to stay that way. She continued to deploy "yes, Harry" to great effect when there was a cause dear to her heart.

Harry led the way to their usual seats, helped Ophelia to hers, and sat in silence as the unexceptional Mr. Drayton spoke of kindness to others, the reward of faith, and the sin of pride.

Harry supposed that the last one was meant for him. He had been quite unabashedly smug when he'd married Ophelia last month. Mr. Drayton had conducted the service, at Ophelia's insistence. She had felt that to have asked anyone else to do the job of marrying them would reflect poorly on the man's reputation. No one but the three of them knew of Drayton's proposal, anyway. Besides, the only alternative was to go to London and be married by special license there. Although expedient, another London trip held no appeal for Harry. He had everything he wanted right there at home.

So he had given in to her request to accommodate Mr. Drayton's pride and bore out another reading of the banns with more patience than he had the first time.

His newfound serenity might have something to do with how often he shared Ophelia's bed. They were rather well-matched in passion. Ophelia enjoyed intimacy in a way few women ever admit to. Nothing he wanted was denied. Everything she desired was his pleasure to grant.

He closed his eyes as the vicar droned on, imagining what

fun might be had between the sheets that night when he took his wife to bed again. He had solved the entire problem of the house's many flights of stairs by moving himself downstairs to *her*. It had taken the servants a week to put things in order, but he now had no reason whatsoever to be far from Ophelia ever again.

They had adjoining bedchambers. They spent almost every night of their marriage together in one of them, or occasionally both.

Ophelia's elbow prodded him, and he opened his eyes to find the vicar glaring at him severely. He wondered briefly just how long he'd been woolgathering that time, and smiled. The other parishioners were looking at them, too, so he assumed he might have even snored. Too bad. He was a duke, and he would only ever have to answer to Ophelia.

"Excellent sermon," he murmured, without regret that he'd missed almost every word spoken of it. His soul did not need saving anymore. Ophelia had it tucked away somewhere about her for safekeeping.

"Indeed."

Ophelia would have stayed awake through the whole of Drayton's droning on. She was a much better person than Harry ever wanted to be.

Harry escorted his wife down the aisle and out into the bright sunshine. Mr. and Mrs. Nash waved at them from a distance, then laughed when he stifled a yawn.

And then Harry noticed Ophelia yawning, too. "We should go."

Ophelia threaded her arm a bit tighter through his. "I think that a very good idea."

Once in the closed carriage, she snuggled into his side. He liked this side of marriage, too. Ophelia seemed to need to be close to him as much as he wanted to be close to her. He still grew aroused by her presence, though now he didn't bother to hide his admiration of her beauty…or his erection.

She rubbed his leg. "You snored again during the service."

Ah, so that explained the vicar's glare. "What can I say? I'm a newly married man with a beautiful wife to blame for keeping me up all night. Isn't it enough that I gave another handsome contribution to the collection plate for his orphans?"

"You were very generous." Ophelia's hand slid higher, halting not far away from his groin. "Do you think we will ever tire of each other?"

He lifted her onto his lap, so she straddled him and then darkened the carriage, so they had privacy. "I can't imagine I will."

"Paul did," she confessed, pulling her skirts out of the way while he unbuttoned the fall of his trousers. Ophelia hardly ever mentioned her first husband, and when she did, it was always a sensitive topic.

He released his cock and settled the tip at her entrance. "I should have met you first."

Ophelia sank down on his length with a soft sigh. "I'm a wicked woman. I thought of doing this all through that boring sermon."

Harry grasped her hips firmly and guided her up and down until they were both panting. He caught her face in one hand, slowing her movements. "I might not say this right, but I am grateful that Paul died. If he hadn't, I might never have been as happy as I am now. I love the wicked woman that you are. I spent the whole sermon planning to make love to you tonight. I'm glad you didn't make me wait until after dinner."

She grabbed him by the hair and turned his head aside. Her teeth nibbled just beneath his ear, and then she whispered, "So, we are as bad as each other?"

"No, we are perfectly right for each other. Let me show you again." He caught her lips with his and kissed her thoroughly, allowing her to move against him at her own pace and with the sway of the carriage. Today she was quick to find her release, and he followed soon after, biting down on her gown to smother the sound of his shout.

Moderating his outbursts was the only sacrifice he'd had to make in marrying Ophelia. Everything else seemed to just fall into place as if they were fated to be together.

Ophelia had once promised that there was one perfect bride who could love him just the way he was. He hadn't thought she'd meant herself at the time...but to his knowledge, it was the only thing she'd ever been mistaken about when it came to love.

PLEASURES OF THE NIGHT

Chapter One

May 1816
London

"Why are you deferring to Sylvia at home? It is not as if she's becoming royalty," Eugenia Hillcrest complained to her youngest cousin as they entered Wharton House, the Marquess of Wharton's grand London mansion in Cavendish Square, after a night of rubbing shoulders with the cream of society.

"Close enough," Aurora noted as she passed off her shawl and reticule to a hovering servant. "Sylvia is to marry one of the most eligible bachelors and popular lords in society. Everyone had been trying to catch his eye until our cousin seduced him."

"She did not seduce him," Eugenia hissed and then moderated her tone down to a whisper. "They fell in love in the best way. Secretly."

"I still cannot believe she didn't say a word to warn us of the blossoming romance, and she should have given us time to prepare for all this," Aurora said, casting a glance up at the vaulted ceiling, where a pastoral scene had recently been painted. Gilt and mirrors, too, as far as the eye could see. "I thought we had a pact to share everything."

Eugenia had thought so, too. But Sylvia had deceived

them both, meeting secretly with a marquess for weeks before they'd both borne witness to the most startling marriage proposal from Lord Wharton. Although annoyed with Sylvia, Eugenia could understand why she had kept her silence about the affair. There were some situations in a woman's life that were impossible to explain properly, especially when one's heart was deeply involved.

The Marquess of Wharton was quite the catch, but he had flaws, too. The first being, he was extremely high-handed. They would never have imagined such a powerful man might be drawn to their dear but poor cousin. But he was utterly besotted with Sylvia. She was glad Wharton had done the honorable thing in the end and proposed a partnership of love and trust.

It helped that Sylvia loved Wharton to distraction, too, and had declared him her perfect match in every way that mattered. Wharton's respect for Sylvia's opinions, even when they were the opposite of his own, had made it easier for Eugenia to accept the match in the end. With Sylvia's marriage into an important family, though, Aurora and Eugenia were both under the continual scrutiny of the unforgiving *ton* forevermore.

And members of the *ton* were easily provoked to spiteful tattling. Even women of her age, seven and twenty, came in for censure for misbehavior, real or imagined, all the time. It was fortunate she had no expectation of making a match herself, but she did worry about spoiling her younger cousin's chances by putting a foot wrong.

A hard rap on the door sounded behind them, and the butler sprang into action to admit a dozen titled gentlemen, wives, and bachelors who had been invited to follow them home. Lord Wharton liked to entertain.

"Ooh, look. More company for tea," Aurora crooned in obvious delight.

Actual tea at this hour of the night tended to be in short supply for Wharton's impromptu parties, but spirits and wine were always plentiful and far more popular.

Eugenia glanced over her shoulder as a pair of late stragglers were admitted. Mr. Thaddeus Berringer, a dark-haired gentleman she'd admired from afar for a while, and Lord Sullivan, a former client of the Hillcrest Academy, strode into the chamber and looked about them, smiling.

Eugenia uttered a happy sigh.

The attendance of the Duke of Exeter's heir would make the evening more enjoyable for her. Good-looking men were meant to be appreciated from all angles and from top to firm-muscled bottom.

She leaned toward her cousin. "Lord Sullivan is here."

Aurora made an unhappy sound but did not turn to see. She had never hidden the fact that she thought little of Lord Sullivan.

Eugenia sighed. "Why can you not be kinder to our former client?"

"I have my reasons," she said loftily.

Sullivan was a nice man. Wealthy. Softly spoken when in the company of ladies. He had not been keen to marry the last time they had met, although he was being pressured by his family. She shrugged away her curiosity about Lord Sullivan's arrival or situation. They were no longer in the business of helping gentlemen prepare to find a bride. Sylvia's engagement had made continuing their work impossible.

She resumed her discreet admiration of Mr. Berringer. "Do you think Exeter's heir has a mistress yet? There is any number of ladies I know trying to catch his eye."

"All the ladies I know who have tried have been soundly rebuffed," Aurora confided.

That made Eugenia even more curious about him. It was no hardship to imagine he could have his pick of lovers. "Married or other?"

"Married," Aurora said with a heavy sigh. "It seems our Mr. Berringer has a severe dislike of becoming an adulterer, and he avoids marriage-minded spinsters, too."

"Society is overrun with both." She chuckled. "Widows will be overjoyed if they figure out they have the best chance of becoming a duchess one day. But I like him all the more for his restraint when it comes to avoiding married women," Eugenia murmured. "I dislike the idea of anyone coming between a couple, even if they are poorly matched."

"Do not disregard the appeal of illicit love," Aurora warned. "He's a man. He'll find someone willing, I'm sure," she said with a decidedly wicked laugh.

He might, too.

Thaddeus Berringer was handsome, of sober habits so far, and a duke's heir. It was widely reported that the Duke of Exeter had settled funds and property on his heir last year. There would be no limit to the vices and scandals he might indulge in one day, if he had the money and the company of wicked friends. He had little influence yet, though, and did not appear overly ambitious. Everyone gossiped over the tiniest details about his days. She had heard he'd left Town two weeks ago, and everyone speculated that there'd been a falling out in the family.

Utterly unfounded, most likely. She had borne witness to the Duke of Exeter and Thaddeus Berringer laughing together with pleasing frequency.

But debutants constantly followed him around ballrooms, hoping to be noticed and singled out for attention. Little was known of his reputation with the ladies at all, which was likely why she found him fascinating.

If he turned out to be as predictable as all other lords in society, Thaddeus Berringer would align himself with a woman of fortune and family in an attempt to gain power and influence over society, even before he became a duke.

They flowed along with everyone else to the drawing room as conversation sprang up between guests. Aurora and Eugenia were largely ignored. They had neither fortune nor fame. Although Sylvia looked their way with an expression of longing, they knew better than to believe she would join them tonight. Wharton talked of politics a great deal at these sorts of things, or he flattered Sylvia outrageously. Neither Eugenia nor Aurora enjoyed such talk for too long, but Sylvia hung on his every word—as it should be.

Besides, there were other topics that interested Eugenia and Aurora, which could entertain them for hours. Their favorite subject would shock prudish members of the *ton*.

Eugenia drew her younger cousin along, circling those gathered. She leaned close to Aurora to whisper, "Who would you have?"

"Tonight…" Aurora pursed her lips briefly, a small smile emerging as they strolled about the chamber considering the choices before them. "I think I should like tall, dark and," her eyes lit up, "mysterious."

Eugenia scanned the crowd again. Tall, dark, and handsome was in plentiful supply. Mr. Berringer was present, and Eugenia's interest had become sadly fixed of late on him—the unobtainable man. But then a new man caught her eye—a stranger to Wharton's late-night gatherings who seemed to match Aurora's description. "I wonder who he could be?"

"Who cares who he is. It's what he can do for a lady that is the real question."

Eugenia hid a smile and discreetly observed the fellow, from the top of his perfectly tousled dark hair to the nicely formed bulge in his black satin breeches. "He seems quite well turned out. Meyer?"

"No, he wears a Weston creation, I believe." Aurora made an approving sound as she twisted a lock of hair around her gloved fingers. "Delightfully fitted garments, one and all. I swear I can estimate his measurements even from here. I wonder if our cousin has the time to introduce us."

Sylvia had her back to them and was laughing in Lord Wharton's company.

"Patience, cousin. Anticipation is half the reward." And it did not do to appear too eager at these sorts of gatherings. Some gentlemen took exception to women they considered forward, and all men gossiped as well as women. If they put a toe out of line, they could find themselves on the outs very quickly with this persnickety set. That might impact Sylvia's standing in society, too.

Aurora pouted. "But am I not deserving of a reward as enticing as he appears to be?"

"Rewards might have to wait until Sylvia is actually married, and we can be ourselves again," Eugenia said, reminding Aurora of their mutual decision to be on their best behavior. Eugenia appreciated a well-proportioned man as much as Aurora did. But the way they had pursued pleasure before Sylvia's engagement was markedly different to how they could do so now.

There were many delights Eugenia had forbidden herself. Dalliances with anyone connected to the Marquess of Wharton's family were a risky venture. She might talk of hope of seduction, but that was as far as she dared imagine for now. And since they mingled almost exclusively with Wharton's set of friends, opportunities for trysts were virtually nonexistent.

A woman joined the mystery man, capturing his arm and full attention. She clung to the man with a proprietary air, so it seemed clear he belonged to some lucky woman. A wife?

Aurora sighed sadly. "Sometimes wondering is more enjoyable than discovering the truth that a man might be married already."

"Indeed, it is." She flashed a conciliatory smile in Aurora's direction. "We can still observe and imagine."

"Indeed, we will, cousin," Aurora promised.

A call rang for everyone to move along to another room where refreshments had been laid out, and they followed with the masses again into the long gallery. After Wharton and Sylvia's engagement had become common knowledge, they had all been pressed to come and live under Wharton's not unsubstantial roof. Not for his benefit but for his mother's health and happiness. Lizzy, the Marchioness of Wharton was still recovering from her breast surgery and remained in a delicate state of health in her chambers upstairs.

They had come along with Sylvia to cheer up the marchioness, distract her from the pain if they could. Neither task was easy, but none of them minded very much. Out of the three of them, Sylvia was most often in her future mama's company. The marchioness had a dry wit Eugenia found compatible with her own, and she didn't mind feeding the older lady harmless tidbits of gossip discovered during their outings.

But their new lives were not confined to sitting by the marchioness' bedside every day. They had been invited to make themselves at home. Sixteen bedchambers, a ballroom, a vast library, a dining room, and a long gallery were now their playground. They were to enjoy themselves at any of

Wharton's impromptu gatherings as if they were family already, too. They could drink and entertain their friends as much as they liked.

Until the marchioness' strength returned, the wedding ceremony had been delayed indefinitely, so they lived in wait for that happy day to come.

Eugenia smiled, knowing her evening was likely bound to be long, but the view always pleasurable. The opulence of the marquess' home had been startling at first, but she'd grown accustomed to gilt everything, and even being introduced to members of the king's family, too. The marquess and his mother kept a large circle of acquaintances from all walks of society, and close friends tended to drop by at all hours.

However, despite Eugenia's love of conversation, she was often relegated to the sidelines due to circumstances beyond her control. First, she was a woman, considered by society as dependent on Wharton's charity because of Sylvia's future elevation to marchioness.

Second, she was considered a bluestocking sort of woman. She had been the driving force behind the Hillcrest Academy —managing the accounting and negotiations for their little enterprise. No one seemed quite sure what to make of their ties to trade. But she had been told that an unmarried cousin of a future marchioness could not possibly earn her own way in the world without facing criticism from all quarters. The Hillcrest Academy was no more.

And third, unfortunately, the best conversations tended to be led by the very same irritating creatures who constantly overlooked that she was more educated than the wealthy debutants they circled. They only asked exceedingly naive debutants of fortune their opinion on any number of topics they could never have knowledge or experience of at their tender ages.

Eugenia possessed a brain and the will to use it. She refused to become a sheep—following nose to tail because she was expected to be like every other lady. She was more intelligent than most debutants and unimpressed by what was considered popular.

As expected, Wharton swept Sylvia into another political debate, leaving Eugenia and Aurora to their own devices as usual.

"There they go," Aurora grumbled. "Forgetting us again."

Eugenia sometimes preferred it that way. An hour with Wharton pontificating on what society needed to do, or stand for, tended to give her a sore head.

Little groups sprang up immediately; gentlemen with their wives and friends attracted most of the bachelors for the present moment. "Would you care for a breath of fresh air, cousin?"

"Yes, indeed I would."

Arm in arm, they sauntered away from all to the quiet end of the long gallery, where a grouping of chairs had been placed beside a window they could open a crack to let in some night air. Eugenia positioned herself directly in the cool draft and signaled to a footman. "Tea, please, Mr. Bloom."

"I've already had it sent for, Miss Hillcrest," he said with a tilt of his ginger head.

"You are a treasure," she enthused, pleased with the new footman's thoughtfulness. "He'll do well if he keeps this up," she whispered to Aurora when he was gone.

Aurora smiled. "I think he is trying to impress you."

"He's the new man below-stairs hoping to make a good impression on all of us to advance his career. If he pleases me, he probably hopes I'll put in a good word for him with the future marchioness." She shrugged, having already made such a recommendation for him to Sylvia a few days ago. "Besides, we're entirely predictable. We always end an evening sipping tea in our corner."

"How terrible to be so predictable."

"We're likely the only ones who are."

They remained on the edge of the crowd in the long gallery, sipping their tea when it came. Happy with their own company and confidences. Though not technically correct for them to remain apart from everyone, they resisted society's rules as often as they could, especially here. Wharton had tried to insist they should have a chaperone when they had first moved under his roof. However, he'd quickly changed his mind when Sylvia had suggested she needed a chaperone now, too.

"Look at them," Aurora whispered.

Eugenia studied the end of the room, where their cousin stood encircled in her future husband's arms. It was a quick embrace, laced with much laughter and tenderness. At home, Wharton could barely keep his hands from his future bride. A chaperone would undoubtedly have gotten in his way.

Eugenia glanced down at her empty teacup and then put it aside. "Still very much in love."

"I hope that never changes," Aurora whispered.

"I'm sure it won't." Eugenia inched closer to her cousin and fluffed out the skirts of her favorite plum-colored gown. She usually favored dark colors, though her family tried to lure her into white or brighter hues. She held on to her individuality as hard as she could. "When two people love each other in that fashion, nothing but death will keep them apart."

"Are you sure?"

She nodded slowly and smiled. "I knew a woman once who proved my point. As a young woman, she was utterly swept off her feet by a man she knew but half a day. She married him by banns a month later and had just one blissful night in his arms as his wife, before he left her."

"This doesn't seem a happy story," Aurora chided.

"It's not, I suppose. When word reached her of his death, she cried for weeks. Bereft and facing a future alone, she could have fallen down and never gotten up again. But that brief love comforts her to this very day. Love, true love, never really dies for the one left behind."

Aurora frowned. "Why did he leave her?"

"She begged him not to," Eugenia swallowed the lump that had suddenly sprung to her throat. Partings were never easy. "He had a mother who waited for his return far away. He was supposed to break the news of his marriage gently, since his mother's health was delicate, and then return to Hastings. But he drowned before he even reached his mother to tell her."

"How sad for both of them. Did they ever meet? The mother and new widow?"

"No. Unfortunately, the lady had been left with insufficient funds. She never did seek out her husband's final resting place to mourn. She wanted to go so very badly, but…"

"What happened to her? The widow. Have you kept in touch with her?"

Eugenia nodded. "She's content. She lives with her cousins."

"Just like us," Eugenia noted.

"Yes, exactly like us." Eugenia didn't like to imagine how her life might have gone on if not for the love and support of her cousins. Together, they had started a new and more exciting life than she'd dreamed.

"I'm glad she had a family to support her," Aurora whispered.

Aurora and Sylvia could never understand how much Eugenia had needed them in her life. "I am, too."

Aurora sighed. "I can't wait to fall in love like them, your friend and Sylvia, I mean."

"You'll be next, I'm sure," Eugenia promised. She ran her eye over the visitors to Wharton House. They were the same men they'd known for almost a year. None had expressed interest in courting Aurora, and Eugenia was disappointed by that. She'd always thought Aurora, being the youngest, would be the first of them to marry, if a marriage was in the cards for any. Aurora was the prettiest and most bubbly of personality, too. Sylvia the most agreeable, while also being the most stubborn.

What society thought of herself, Eugenia had no idea…but she hoped they didn't ever inquire too deeply into her past.

More Regency Romance...

DISTINGUISHED ROGUES SERIES

Chills ~ Broken ~ Charity ~ An Accidental Affair

Keepsake ~ An Improper Proposal ~ Reason to Wed

The Trouble with Love ~ Married by Moonlight

Lord of Sin ~ The Duke's Heart ~ Romancing the Earl

One Enchanted Christmas ~ Desire by Design

His Perfect Bride ~ Pleasures of the Night ~ Silver Bells

Seduced in Secret ~ Yours Until Dawn

No Ordinary Lady ~ Miss Kimble Bites Back

SCANDALOUS BRIDES SERIES

Wicked with Him

Desperately Seeking Seduction

Love and Other Disasters

Surrender Becomes Her

WILD RANDALLS SERIES

Engaging the Enemy ~ Forsaking the Prize

Guarding the Spoils ~ Hunting the Hero

*

SAINTS AND SINNERS SERIES

The Duke and I ~ A Gentleman's Vow

An Earl of Her Own ~ The Lady Tamed

*

REBEL HEARTS SERIES

The Wedding Affair ~ An Affair of Honor

The Christmas Affair ~ An Affair so Right

*

MISS MAYHEM SERIES

Miss Watson's First Scandal

Miss George's Second Chance

Miss Radley's Third Dare

Miss Merton's Last Hope

About Heather Boyd

USA Today Bestselling Author Heather Boyd believes every character she creates deserves their own happily-ever-after—no matter how much trouble she puts them through. With that goal in mind, she writes steamy romances that skirt the boundaries of propriety to keep readers enthralled until the wee hours of the morning. Heather has published over fifty regency romance novels and shorter works full of daring seductions and distinguished rogues. She lives north of Sydney, Australia, with her trio of rogues and a four-legged overlord.

Find out more about Heather at:
Heather-Boyd.com

facebook.com/HeatherBoydRomanceAuthor

instagram.com/heatherboydbooks

bookbub.com/authors/heather-boyd

goodreads.com/Heather_Boyd